Spring Into SciFi

2018 Edition

Foreword by Andrew M. Ferrell

With Stories From:
Sandy Stuckless
Anthony Engebretson
Desmond Warzel
Tony Conaway
Ewan R. Chapman
Mike Adamson
Myke Edwards
Matthew McKiernan
Nick Morrison
John Haas
Nick Korolev
Kate E. Lore
Larry Lefkowitz

GW00771294

Cover Designed by:
    Steger Productions
https://stegerproduction.wixsite.com/design

Published by:
Cloaked Press, LLC
PO Box 341
Suring, WI 54174

http://www.cloakedpress.com

ISBN-10: 0-9991690-1-7
ISBN-13: 9780999169018
Library of Congress Control Number: 2018930172

First Edition: March 2018

Foreword

Science Fiction, a genre that conjures up many images for any fan. Epic space battles with beautifully crafted worlds, their denizens running the gamut of humanoid to whatever the writer dreamed up. Or maybe it is advanced robotics and cybernetics against the backdrop of a technologically superior society. No matter what brings you to the realm of sci-fi, I think we have something here for you.

Our authors have come together to present their unique takes on the genre for you. They brought their aliens, their space travel, advanced technology, artificial intelligence, and even some time travel. We hope you will enjoy what they have to offer.

Andrew M. Ferrell
Founder of Cloaked Press
Author of Beginnings, "Family Heritage Volume 1"

Table of Contents

Date Night
by Sandy Stuckless

The targeting reticle in Tobias Rana's right eye locked onto her face from the other side of the street, and he smiled. Even in this horrid weather, with her strawberry blond hair matted to the side of her face, she was beautiful. He wasn't supposed to think like that, but how could he not? He'd never seen anyone like her. Too bad she only had an hour to live.

Rain drummed down on his head. He crossed the street as vehicles sped overhead, the jet wash pulling waves of icy water over him. There was a hitch in his step; a nervousness he'd never felt before. Tobias ducked into a narrow laneway next to the restaurant and, with a twitch of his left index finger, pulled up the diagnostics for his cybernetics. No problems listed. His was a purely human reaction.

He shook off the inconvenient weakness, not wanting it to interfere with the evening's schedule. None of it mattered. All that mattered was her. He thought about using his direct link into the Network to look her up, but changed his mind. He didn't approve of pre-meeting surveillance. He didn't need to know about her family, her dog, or her job. The personal background only provided opportunities to form attachments. That was the last thing he wanted. Still, she was lovely.

The only thing he needed to know was her name.

Sarah.

That's what the contract said.

From what he could see of her, she didn't have any cybernetics. It was a bit odd, but strangely refreshing. Tobias wished he didn't need the implants himself, but they were the only way he could do his job. They were also the only thing keeping him alive.

And this was a high-profile job. Double his normal fee, plus he'd received all of the latest upgrades to ensure nothing went wrong. The Network was serious about this one.

He moved his left pinky finger slightly. Pale pink skin rose from his wrist, revealing a compartment embedded in his arm. The vial was still there, waiting to be deployed when he was ready. It was not that time yet. He needed to be patient and let the evening play out a little first. It wouldn't kill him to learn a bit about her.

She was early for their date by almost fifteen minutes. A coincidence, maybe, or was she worried about her safety? He wouldn't be surprised if it were the latter. She seemed like an intelligent lady. The Network didn't send people like him after the dumb ones.

He waited five minutes after she entered the restaurant before following. He needed her to feel as comfortable and confident as possible. Comfortable and confident people let their guard down and made mistakes.

The first thing he noticed when he entered the foyer was her perfume. Sweet and fruity pleasantness. Pears, unless he missed his guess. Tobias turned down his olfactory enhancers a little. Just enough to push the scent to the background.

"Sarah?" He offered his warmest smile. "I'm Tobias. You're even prettier than your profile picture let on."

She brushed a wisp of hair behind her ear

and accepted his outstretched hand with a shy smile. "Thank you. It's nice to meet you."

She was still nervous. Not unusual, but it wouldn't do. He couldn't fathom why the Network was so adamant on eliminating her. Perhaps he should've done a little surveillance. "Shall we get a table and order some drinks? I could use one after the day I've had." He turned to the maître d'. "A table in one of your private rooms, please. I expect not to be disturbed."

The maître d' bowed slightly. "Of course, sir. Right this way."

Tobias tilted his head from side to side, scanning the layout of the restaurant as the maître d' showed them to a room. They were light on covers tonight. Only eight other diners in the restaurant. Counting the serving staff, there would be no more than twenty people in the building. If he could keep it quiet, there was no reason why they should be a factor.

Tobias waited for Sarah to set her purse on the table before relieving her of her dripping jacket. He nearly dropped it on the floor at the sight of the stunning woman beneath. He clicked his jaw shut before she noticed. The knee-length dress hugged her lithe form, showing off all of her curves.

"This weather is something else, hey?" he asked, to change his train of thought. He couldn't let her beauty distract him, as difficult as that would be. His cybernetics gave him a list of topics to bring up, but he didn't need them. This wasn't the first date he'd been on.

"I hate it. It always puts me in a bad mood. I'm not like most people who rely on cybernetics to tell them how to feel."

Tobias couldn't tell if that was a direct jab at him or not. "Oh, I don't know. Cybernetics aren't all bad. I've learned to live with mine over time."

Sarah bit her lower lip and her cheeks reddened slightly. "I'm sorry. No offence intended. I just don't believe in human augmentation."

"None taken," Tobias replied, "but I'm curious to learn more of your opinions."

The waiter came by and took their order

for a bottle of the house white. Tobias listened as she recited how she thought humanity was being lost to the machines. "It's like a street drug," she said. "People can't get enough."

That explained why the Network wanted her eliminated. Beliefs alone weren't enough to turn a whole corporation against someone, though. What had she done to piss them off?

"I hope you don't mind me asking. How did you get your cybernetics?"

Tobias leaned back in his chair and rubbed the back of his neck. "I had little choice, really. I got caught up in the civil war and an explosion left me with just a torso and a brain. It wasn't a hard decision to make."

"I see," she said and sipped her wine. "You're different than most people. Many of them do have a choice, yet they still elect to augment their bodies. Usually more for someone else's benefit than their own."

"How do you mean?"

"Isn't it obvious?" she replied. "Employers want better workers, spouses want better lovers.

Nobody is good enough as they were made anymore."

There was some truth to what she said. He wondered if perhaps there was something more personal behind her statements. "I won't deny that my life is vastly different because of the augments. Better in some ways, not so much in others."

Sarah rubbed her fingers over the back of her hand. "I actually admire you, Tobias. You still think for yourself, outside of the Network. You see your augments as tools instead of as a part of you."

Tobias's wine glass paused halfway to his mouth. "Why can't they be both? Your hand is a tool to eat your food, to drink your wine, to open doors, yet it is still a part of you."

She cracked a thin smile. "Yes, I suppose you have a point, but there's still a difference. Most people now see only the augments, and forget everything that makes them human."

"On that, my dear, we can agree." He held her gaze a little longer before she bit her lower lip and looked away.

Tobias scanned her biometrics; heart rate down, pulse steady, not sweating, though he didn't need the scanner to see the last one. She was beginning to relax. A bit longer and he could complete his job.

A pang of...something...fluttered in his belly. Almost like butterflies, but even less pleasant. Disappointment. Yes, that had to be it. The message on his reticle confirmed the reason behind it. It was the Network. *Payment transfer complete. Activate mission protocol.*

Tobias didn't want to. Not yet. He was enjoying the evening and the conversation was stimulating.

The waiter returned, and Sarah even let him order for her. After ensuring she liked seafood, Tobias settled on the lemon pepper salmon for the both of them. The waiter left and his reticle flashed again.

Activate mission protocol.

Tobias at least wanted to eat his salmon first before carrying out that order. He topped up their wine glasses and prepared to continue their discussion on lost humanity. It had been some time since he'd enjoyed such conversation.

"I know you're here to kill me, Tobias. I'm not stupid. You're basically a walking advertisement for the Network, and they want me gone."

Tobias grinned to himself. He'd been right about her. She was intelligent. "Why did you agree to meet me then? You must know you've made my job easier."

It occurred to him then that maybe it was she who had lured him here. It didn't make sense that a high-profile target of the Network would engage in online dating. "You set it all up, didn't you? I should've seen it sooner. My own fault, I guess, for getting drawn in by your good looks."

Sarah shrugged. "Human nature is still human nature, even if you are half robot."

Her hand shot to her mouth in embarrassment, but Tobias let the mild insult go. She wasn't really wrong.

The waiter brought their meal and retreated from the room once again. The lemon scent overpowered her perfume, and Tobias turned up his olfactory enhancers to smell it again. He tucked the cloth napkin into his shirt and started in on the salmon. It came as advertised. Delicious. "You still haven't told me why you picked me."

She poked the rice with her fork and wouldn't look up at him. "When I placed the ad, I wasn't targeting you specifically, but I knew someone from the Network would respond. I wanted to see if I could change their mind." She put down her utensils and picked up the wine glass. She offered him a slight, almost inviting smile. "Perhaps you would be willing to help me instead."

Tobias stopping chewing. "You couldn't even if they wanted to change their minds. The protocols in my operating system keep me from deviating. If it's any consolation, I don't want to kill you."

A small glimmer of hope flashed in her bright emerald eyes. "What happens if you try to deviate?"

"Let's put it this way: one of us is leaving here dead tonight."

Sarah studied him with intense eyes and Tobias shifted in his seat, suddenly uncomfortable in his own right. "How were you planning on doing it?"

Tobias let out a slow breath through his nose. This was highly unorthodox. He didn't like talking openly about his work, especially to a victim. But then again, nothing about his evening had been orthodox.

"Please," she pressed. "I deserve at least that much."

Tobias held out his wrist and the compartment opened, revealing the vial of cyanide. "I was going to spike your food with it when you went to powder your nose. I guess that's out of the question now, isn't it?"

She rubbed the back of her hand, seemly unnerved. It served her right. She had asked, after all.

"What if I told you it didn't have to be that way? What if I told you there was a way out for both of us? Would you take it?"

That question was harder to answer than

she realized. The Network had given him his life back, but sometimes he hated what they made him do with it. What little conscience he had left struggled with that daily.

The three words continued to flash on his reticle.

Activate mission protocol. Activate mission protocol. Activate mission protocol.

Still, he did not. "Tell me about your way out," he said. Not because he expected to take it, but because he was genuinely curious. This was not the way he typically behaved with targets, but something compelled him to alter his routine.

She picked at the salmon, taking small bites. "I assume by your earlier statement that you are aware of the Apocalypse Protocol?"

"I didn't know it had a name, but yes, I know of it. It's to keep mission-ready units on task if things go to hell and the link to the Network is lost."

"Yes and no. There's one thing you're missing. At any given moment, the Network can take control of your body and use it as a weapon, whether you want it to or not."

Tobias wiped his mouth and dropped the napkin into his lap. "That seems a bit extreme."

"That's not even the whole of it. Every single person with a Network cybernetic has this protocol. Even if it's just a time piece embedded in your wrist."

Tobias set down his fork and knife and picked up his water goblet. For the first time in a long while, his hand trembled. "You're saying everyone is walking around with this kill switch wired into them? Why would the Network do that?"

"They want their own personal army of assassins. You are nothing more than a weapon to them. To be discarded when your usefulness has run out."

Tobias shouldn't have cared, except for the fact that it made him redundant. If the Network could use anyone as an assassin, why did they need him? He'd be sure to ask them when he delivered his report.

A sharp pain stabbed through his temple

and he clamped his eyes shut. The message on the reticle had changed. *Complete the contract.*

Without any conscious input, his operating system went through the combat sequences and selected strangulation. He was stronger than her. She would be easy to overpower. He clenched his hands shut against the urge to leap across the table at her.

"Are you okay?" Sarah asked. She seemed genuinely concerned for him, but her heart rate was elevated again and her skin flushed. Her right hand grasped the silver knife tightly. She wasn't concerned for his well-being. She was worried for her own.

Tobias's fingers danced as he went through the program and deactivated the protocol, but it was only a temporary solution. "They're getting impatient."

"Should I run?"

"It would do you no good," he replied simply. It wasn't a boast on his part. He had chosen the vial to eliminate her, but there were a hundred ways he could do it before she even made it to the front door. He took a deep breath. "Keep talking. You said you had a way out. What is it?"

"I've developed a subroutine to target and isolate the protocol."

"That's impossible," Tobias replied. The pain intensified and, once again, the message changed. *Do it now*. The strangulation protocol reactivated and the *Engage* prompt on his reticle flashed green.

"I can prove it. I have the subroutine with me. We could try it."

Tobias barked a short laugh. The ridiculous idea she had suggested was beyond the pale. "Let me get this straight. You want me to plug a strange subroutine into my operating system in hopes of shutting down some fabled kill switch protocol, and you don't even know if it works?"

"The Apocalypse Protocol is not fabled."

"How do you know? Give me one good reason to believe any of this."

"I'm the one who created it. I know its mapping, its overrides, everything."

"Why would you do that? And why are you

trying to stop it now that it's out?"

"I thought I was developing it for unmanned combat units in defense contracts. When I found out the Network planned to implement it across the board, I started working secretly on the off switch, Phoenix."

"But you were found out before you could test it."

"I barely escaped with my life. I haven't been able to test Phoenix, but I know it works. I just need a chance to prove it."

Tobias scanned her biometrics again, but mostly read her body language. He found no indication that she was lying. Everything she said, she believed. It didn't mean he was ready to let her introduce strange code into his operating system. "Okay, Sarah, you have me intrigued. Not entirely convinced, but intrigued. I'm going to try to buy us some time while we figure out what do next."

Tobias pulled up the mission protocol file, but there was something wrong. The kill order wasn't where it normally was. He dug deeper into his operating protocols and found a file he couldn't access. Never before had he been locked out of a file in his own operating system.

Tobias wasn't impressed. He didn't care if the Network had provided the implants. This was still his mind and he would keep control of it.

He pulled up the main operating system file and searched for the file access subroutine. The code had been changed. He tried to change it back, but his access was denied.

The reticle flashed again. *Do not deviate. Complete the mission.*

Like hell, he thought. Suddenly, everything Sarah had told him seemed not only possible, but entirely plausible. He tried to alter the code in his operating system again, and this time the response was more severe.

Tobias's hands clenched tightly as pain stabbed through his temples and into his forehead. His stomach turned and the salmon he'd eaten almost became an accessory on Sarah's pretty dress. What the hell was this? No control over his own programming? That just wasn't going to fly with him.

The waiter entered their private room. Only, he wasn't carrying a fresh bottle of the house white. He carried a meat cleaver. His eyes locked on Tobias and he never slowed on his way to their table.

"I don't think he's coming to offer us dessert," Sarah said as she pushed her chair away from the table.

Tobias scanned through his combat protocols. Surprise would be the best. He clutched the polished silver knife in his left hand. The waiter raised the cleaver, but Tobias was too fast for him. He leapt, burying the knife deep into the waiter's throat.

The cleaver fell to the floor as the red ichor flowed down Tobias's hand and left dark trails in the pressed blue fabric of his shirtsleeves. Tobias sank back into his chair and pressed his palm to his temple. "We don't have a lot of time. Show me this subroutine."

Sarah fished into her purse for something while Tobias fought the intensifying agony in his head. It felt like someone was drilling through his skull.

The door to the room opened again, alerting him that more danger was coming. A skinny, clumsy-looking patron and the sous chef in his stained white coat entered from the front of the restaurant, each carrying a gleaming carving knife. There was no mistaking their intent.

Sarah had pushed herself farther away from the table in a panic, dropping her purse to the floor in the process. The cleaver the waiter had carried lay next to his body. Tobias retrieved it and struggled to his feet. It was getting harder to resist the Network's commands. Blood splattered over the tables and floor as he dealt with the patron and the cook. "Hurry up, Sarah. I don't know how much longer I can keep this up."

Before Sarah could get to him with Phoenix, two more patrons stormed into the room. This time it was a woman in business attire and a burly fellow that could've been a security guard or even a cop. Tobias hated killing women, and cops were always a challenge.

Tobias fought the nausea and pain. His movements were sluggish. He took down the man with a quick swipe of the cleaver across his neck, but the woman was a different story.

She fought with precision and grace. With the Network downloading combat sequences into her implants, she matched him strike for strike. He wrestled the carving knife from her hand and pinned her to the ground. As he fought off pain and control impulses from the Network, he snapped her neck, killing her instantly.

Five dead--so much for doing this quietly. There were still at least twelve potential killers in this building. Tobias couldn't fight them all and his programming at the same time.

Tobias rolled off of the woman's corpse and onto his back. This wasn't what he'd signed up for. He shouldn't be killing innocents. The Network would call them collateral damage, but he didn't like to work that way. Tobias needed to stop this now before things got worse.

"Is there any way to upload Phoenix right to the Network and shut down this thing in everybody?"

"I wouldn't be very good at my job if there weren't. I just need to get it into one host and it will replicate through all of them. I think."

Not exactly the confidence boost he was

hoping for, but it would have to do.

A chair flew over their heads, smashing to pieces against the wall. Glass from the light fixtures and other delicate décor showered down onto them.

Tobias scrambled behind the table on his hands and knees. He overturned it, sending wine, salmon, and dishes to the floor, then pulled Sarah down behind it.

He pulled his pant leg up past his knee and opened another compartment hidden in a limb. His practiced hands had the hidden pistol assembled and loaded in under thirty seconds.

"You brought a gun to our date?" Sarah said in shocked dismay.

"Uh, yeah. Assassin, remember?" He peeked out around the edge of the table. His infrared scanners identified four heat signatures. There were probably others he couldn't see. "I always like to have a solid Plan B available, just in case."

Without warning, Tobias popped up from behind the table. He tracked the pistol from left to right, squeezing off three quick shots. The thud of three bodies hitting the floor followed. Tobias hoped they had enjoyed their last meal.

"I need my purse," Sarah cried. "Phoenix is in my purse."

Tobias shifted out around the table, going to deal with the rest of the threats. "Stay here. I'll get it."

Before he'd even cleared the table, a high-pitched squeal erupted in his ears and pain like he'd never felt before knocked him to the floor. The gun fell from his hand and he couldn't move. The Network had stepped up their attacks on him.

Tobias convulsed on the floor for a minute before everything stopped. Through a haze of pain, he saw Sarah cowering in the corner, a steak knife as her only means of defense. It would do her no good.

His reticle flickered.

Restart Mode: Activated.

Apocalypse Mode: Engaged.

That wasn't good. The Network was taking control of his implants. Soon, he'd be nothing more than a passenger in his own body. Here was the true horror of Sarah's Apocalypse Protocol.

Tobias rolled over onto his stomach so that he was facing Sarah. He held out his arm and opened the compartment in his wrist. "You're running out of time, Sarah." The words came through a strained voice. "I'm losing control. Take the vial and stick it in my heart. It will kill me."

She shook her head. "I can't. I won't."

"If you want to live, you will. There is nothing more I can do."

She dropped the steak knife and moved from the corner to retrieve her purse. "There is something I can do. I can still deploy Phoenix."

"It's too late. The Network has already commandeered my operating system. Once I reboot, they will have complete control." Tobias ejected the vial onto the floor in front of her. "Take it."

She looked from Tobias to the vial, fear and doubt on her face. She reached for the canister containing the pale blue liquid, but her hand hesitated.

"Go on," Tobias urged. "You can do it."

She let out a slow breath and picked up the vial. "Only as a last resort. I still want to try Phoenix."

Tobias rotated his head to the right. "There's a port behind my left ear. It links directly into my cortex. If it's going to work, that's your best chance."

Tobias opened the cover and she plugged the data drive in. The download took less than a second and the effect took even less. Pain exploded in his head, his chest, his arms, and his legs. It felt like he was coming apart at the seams. Sarah might not need to use the vial to kill him. Phoenix might do the job for her.

The reticle went dark. His whole vision went dark. There wasn't even a silhouette of Sarah. He couldn't see anything. Come to think of it, he couldn't feel anything either.

Everything that was keeping him alive was shutting down. It seemed his premonition of one of them leaving here dead was about to come true. Sarah's chances of survival had taken their own serious hit.

Tobias let himself go. He wouldn't call it freedom. Death wasn't really a way out, but at least it was an ending. A satisfying one, perhaps. This wasn't exactly the way he'd envisioned it, but he had always expected it to be violent in some manner.

The end did not come, though. His reticle came back online with a flashing cursor awaiting some input. There was a basic operating system in his memory somewhere. One without all the bells and whistles of his assassin's protocol.

It took a moment, but Tobias found and initiated the operating system file he needed. He sucked in a deep breath as his respirator engaged. That was a good thing, he figured. His optical receptors came back online and filmy light filtered through his eyes. Next, his legs twitched. He wasn't sure he could use them, but at least he could feel them again. The same for his arms.

"Tobias! Tobias! Can you hear me?"

The voice sounded distant, muffled, but also familiar. What was going on here?

His vision cleared a bit more and he saw a beautiful woman kneeling over him, shaking him.

Her lips moved. She was the source of the familiar voice.

His operating system was finally fully loaded and functioning. All systems were online. Maybe there was something in his memory banks that could tell him who this woman was and what had happened.

It seemed like his luck was good. All of his memory files were still intact, and after a brief moment, the system rebooted. The whole evening came flooding back like a tsunami.

He smiled at Sarah as she helped him sit up. He raked his fingers through his hair and peered around her at the bodies and the blood. "There's a few more there now."

She laughed. "Turns out I'm not a bad shot." She held out the gun to him. "I believe this is yours."

Tobias took the gun and turned it over in his hands. "Doesn't look like I'll be needing it any more."

She sank to the floor beside him. "How much do you remember?"

"Everything, now that my memory banks have been restored. Including how much I liked your perfume. Pear, right?"

She laid a hand gently on his cheek and smiled. "What about all the other stuff?"

"I can't access any of my assassin protocols, if that's what you're asking. All the combat sequences have been deactivated. Like you said, Phoenix worked."

Sarah helped him to his feet. Everything seemed to be back to normal. "What do you say we get out of here and go somewhere for a drink," she said. "This place is dead anyway."

Tobias laughed as he led her to the front door and out onto the rainy street.

Sandy Stuckless writes in fantasy, sci-fi, and a little paranormal. He enjoys outdoorsy stuff like camping, hiking, and throwing snowballs at his kids. He lives with his family in Toronto.

To learn more about Sandy and his work, connect with him at:
Twitter: @SandyRStuckless
Facebook:
https://www.facebook.com/SandyRStuckless

The Portal
By Anthony Engebretson

145 pounds.

Up one pound from yesterday.

What did I do wrong?

There was a body mirror right next to the scale. I checked my naked form for what would be the first of many times that day. My upper body looked slender enough: my shoulder blades protruded and my ribs were slightly visible; in general, my torso was on the level of an athletic 12-year-old despite me being 25. My face was gaunt and boyish and my skin pale brown. My curly hair was thinning; since high school, I used to be able to grow one hell of a goatee, but now I was only able to get a barely noticeable five o'clock shadow.

My lower half told a different story. My legs and thighs appeared massive to me and my stomach looked bloated as it always felt. I could swear those old white stretch marks from years back were expanding.

I felt an uncomfortable hum in my gut. These brief hums were the only way I could tell the portal was there.

I slipped on my white tank top and grey sweatpants and sat on the sterile twin bed to check my phone.

No new texts. The night before, my buddy, Brandon, was giving me updates on the Chiefs vs. Raiders game since I had no other way to follow it here. The damn Raiders won. I looked at the last bit of our exchange.

Brandon: *If we had an actual fucking defense I dunno*

Me: *We gotta go down 2 a game again someday. We might be good luck charms LOL*

He didn't respond. I wished he did.

I left the tiny room and made my way down the hallway. The building reminded me of an orthodontist's office. It had a woody, Home Depot smell from remodeling and tacky tan walls with paintings of bowls of fruit and vast green pastures. The doors to the other bedrooms were always closed; I never saw any other subjects around, even in the cafeteria. In fact, the halls were almost always empty. I wondered if staff came in from a different entrance. I made my way toward the office of Emily Andre, the project director.

Her door was wide open. She sat at her two computer monitors; the one on her right was facing away from me. The larger one on her left was slightly turned so I could see the scenic Grand Canyon background. When she saw me, her crooked mouth stretched into a broad, warm grin.

"Good morning, James!" she said in a sing-song tone.

I nodded silently. Today she wore a silk grey dress that showed her defined and toned body. The woman looked like Serena Williams. I always felt inadequate around her, and the portal let off a hum that made me queasy.

She stretched her arm to the chair in front of her. I declined.

"I went up a pound."

She stood up. "Have you been sticking with the diet plan?"

"Yeah."

She nodded and gently stroked her silky black hair, thinking.

"Well, you know, what we could do is turn up the intensity a bit." She put her hands on her hips, which complemented her talk-show host tone. "Totally up to you, of course. But if you want to, we should probably do it before you eat breakfast."

I could smell breakfast from the small cafeteria near her office: pancakes and hash browns. My stomach grumbled before the portal overwhelmed it with a sickening hum.

"What's a bit?"

"Let's see, right now the portal consumes about 1/5 of your caloric intake. Maybe we can bump that up to 2/5?"

31

She shrugged and puffed out her lower lip in a playful frown as if it was no big deal. Without thinking about it, I copied her mannerism. "Okay."

She smiled and strutted past me, motioning for me to follow behind her. We made our way down the hall on the opposite side of the subject quarters. At the far end were double doors leading to the portal development lab.

In my freshman year of high school, I was overweight and well on my way to being obese. While I got along with a lot of kids in school and was generally well liked, there were still enemies who'd called me "tubby" or "fat ass". Even my buddies affectionately called me "big boy" and in JV football, I was nicknamed "The Rhino".

I decided I didn't want to be fat. This is America; land of the obesity epidemic and the rest of the world utterly disgusted by us. I couldn't be part of that statistic.

So I dieted and exercised religiously and got myself to a healthy weight. But I was always terrified of becoming fat again. I became a vegetarian and tried diets like the Paleo, Atkins, Dukan, Weight Watchers, Volumetrics – you name it. My friends heckled me for every one. I never stuck to them, mainly because they were just too expensive and complicated.

Besides, all I wanted was to get myself to a point where I could live my life not having to worry about my weight or food.

One day I was looking through the newspaper trying to find a job. I had no heart or energy to continue pursuing a master's degree and I needed money. My parents cut me off; they wanted me to come live with them for a while. They never failed to express concern whenever they saw me. They thought I was depressed or worse. Those discussions would always end with me telling them to drop it or I'm leaving. I figured, when the hell did they decide to be supportive?

When I was overweight, they were the ones who made me feel the worst. There were too many dinners where Dad took a look at my plate and muttered, "Don't you think that's a bit much?" Or Mom would prod me about how I was "getting a bit big". The worst was when they bought me an exercise ball for Christmas.

The paper flashed disgusting ads for "Cheeritos - Cheeto stuffed burritos", "Chocolate pancake sausage burgers" and "triple berry blast soda", paralleled with pictures of chiseled men and women in ads for fad diets and exercises like "500 calorie diet!", "Make your food look gross with the vision diet!" and "Go to bed hungry! Wake up beautiful!"

The ad that really caught my eye was beneath an article about a Chinese Multinational Food manufacturing company, Huàn Xióng, which was developing some new nutritional paste called ReFo. It was a cheap, slimy substance that would be distributed worldwide.

The ad was small and far from flashy and read:

"Want *control of your weight* and *your life*? Subjects needed to test a new weight management procedure.

Must be at least 18 years of age and in a normal to overweight weight range. Subjects who successfully complete this trial will be *paid $10,000.*

7221 Yankee Hill Drive. The Delambre Corporation. *No More Questions.*"

The whole operation was located in a mini-mall toward the outskirts of the city. It was a '70s era brown brick building. I had to sign 15 different liability forms after they explained the procedure.

The company was developing portal technology. Emily felt they could combine this technology with her dream of a new weight management system. They explained everything to me. Miniature portals were deemed safe enough to sit within a human stomach. The portals functioned similarly to black holes, in that they used a miniature pull to consume food particles. These particles were then transported and processed elsewhere.

They showed me videos explaining the process, showing imagery of beautiful and thin people playing on the beach; they also showcased successful animal subjects like a dog that never gained weight despite being given dozens of treats as well as meals. I was also shown an illustration: Picture A depicted one portal snuggled inside a stomach consuming little cubes to represent food particles, and Picture B, where those particles were dropped into a processing chamber. Emily went out of her way to convince me this is exactly what I want, what I need; without this I'll have to spend the rest of my life fretting over what I'm eating. I even failed to question the legality of such a program, as Delambre seemed to be a private organization rather than government-funded.

The little voice that told me this was a terrible idea sat in its corner like a good boy.

The procedure went smoothly. I'd had the portal for a week. I thought progress was being made, my weight was going down! But now I was up one pound again. It was time to turn up its intensity.

We entered the Lab, where the white-coated technicians were tinkering with the massive laser gun-like machine, as if they expected me. They sat me in the chair and stuck me with a needle. I dizzied and blacked out. They needed to put patients to sleep because, while quick, the portal procedure could be painful and even traumatic. After what felt like two seconds, I woke up groggily to Emily's grin.

"Success!"

Fantastic.

I went on to gobble down my breakfast: fruit, hash browns, and pancakes with plenty of butter and syrup. I downed it with a sack of milk with the raccoon-faced Huàn Xióng logo on it. That company probably provided all our food. I was ravenous until I saw Emily watching me from the doorway with her "Good Morning America" smile. The portal gave a queasy hum and I pushed my plate away.

A couple weeks went by and my weight went down to 135 pounds. Even though I was getting thinner, paler, and weaker, my heart leaped every time I checked it. The portal gave off a warm and ticklish hum.

Mom and Dad each tried to call me about 10 times. I didn't answer, nor did I know what they wanted as they never left texts or voicemails. They probably just wondered where I was.

Emily looked pleased. I asked her once if I was getting too low.

"Are you consuming the amount of calories we wanted you to eat?" Her tone framed it like a rhetorical question.

"Yes." I actually wasn't lying.

"Well, it should be balancing out. Maybe we'll up it a tiny bit. Remember, how much you lose, gain or maintain is in your control."

I was having difficulty sleeping, constantly waking up with my mind racing. Sometimes I would get anxiety attacks out of absolutely nowhere, as if an invisible lion was in the room. In other times I would slip into deep bouts of sadness and emptiness. During these times, I found myself hoping I would grow so skeletally thin that I just would die in my sleep. All the while, despite how thin I got, I was still haunted by the heavy bloated gut.

One morning, I made my way to the bathroom, enraged and panicked because my weight had gone up to 137 for some reason. An angry and painful hum bellowed from the portal.

Was it that cheesecake? Too much? Maybe it was those grapes I had between lunch and supper? Why did I do that? That was so stupid!

The facility bathroom was across from Emily's office. Her door was open and her light was on, but she was nowhere to be found. On one of the monitors I noticed the illustration they had showed me when I first came here: Picture A showed the portal in the stomach eating cube shaped "food particles". Picture B displayed another portal dropping them into a processing portal. Picture C...

I never knew there was a Picture C. I looked around; the facility was empty as always. I went into Emily's office. There was an uneasy feeling that I wasn't where I belonged, like a sneaky peasant sitting on a king's throne. Still, I looked at the illustration more closely.

Picture C showed the food in the processing chamber being ground up. I was surprised to find there was also a Picture D. It illustrated the processed food coming out of a machine on a tread, in the form of a liquid sludge. I had no idea what I was looking at. I was startled by the "You Got Mail" ping from her Outlook on the other computer. The new email was from the Huàn Xióng company.

Ms. Andre,
Increasing the portal's intake has proven to be far more efficient in paste production. Thank you for fulfilling our request.

Xi Yuán
Huàn Xióng Incorporated

Paste production? Paste. A shudder electrified my spine when I remembered the blurb about the ReFo nutritional paste.

I looked up and noticed Emily casually standing in the door. She had a good humored smile on her face and she giggled.

"James? What are you doing? Wanna do my job today?"

"My food is being made into paste?"

Emily's smile dropped into a crooked frown. It seemed to me like her entire face transformed and her expression became stern.

"Yes." Her voice was deeper.

"That people will eat?"

She nodded.

"Why didn't you tell me?"

"Was it really necessary? Who cares?"

"I do!" I gagged. I felt violated. It was like people would be eating my shit.

"Okay. Picture this, James. There are millions of people in the world who want to be thinner or at least they want to maintain a healthy weight, right?" She slowly walked toward me. "Then there are billions more who just need to be fed. Period. The number is growing every day, but we don't have enough food!"

She came close and stood over me. I never realized before that she was slightly taller than me.

"In nature things cycle and recycle all the time. Why can't we humans do that with our food? We and Huàn Xióng have set out to create a world where the haves can be as thin as they like and the have-nots can be fed. Everybody can be happy."

She put her hands on my bony shoulders. She was putting slight pressure on them. She smiled and her tone bubbled up again.

"You had no idea you were so important, did you?"

I looked down and shook my head. This wasn't what I wanted. I was thinking about my body more than ever now. I felt like Delambre saw me not as a human being they wanted to help, but a machine. A queasy hum vibrated within me.

"You should tell people before they…"

"Why? People are selfish. They don't understand the things that need to be done to ensure we can survive a changing world."

A jab of guilt hit my gut. She lifted my chin up so I could look into her piercing hazel eyes.

Her tone lowered again and her words struck like a cobra. "You can get the portal removed and go home empty-handed. But you will never have control of your weight or your life and you know it! So, what'll it be?"

I decided she was right; the only problem was that I couldn't get over myself. I nodded complacently.

She smiled a warm mother's smile. "Let's get you some breakfast, shall we?"

That evening, I was making my way to the cafeteria when I heard a woman's high, boisterous voice in the reception area, shouting. "What do you mean I don't have permission to see him!? Do I need permission to knock your damn head off?"

There was also a soft male murmur trying to calm her down.

Recognizing these voices, I came into the reception area. There, a thick squat woman was chewing out the terrified elderly receptionist accompanied by the voice of Bob Seger. Next to her stood a lanky, pale shy man. When the woman saw me, her eyes widened with horror.

Her voice softened, "Baby. Oh god, what did they do to you?"

"Mom, Dad, what are you doing here?"

"Brandon told us you were here," Dad said softly.

Mom burst in, "What the hell are you thinking, James? You didn't need to lose any more weight!"

"I'm fine. I'm not trying to lose anything." Putting on my pathetic poker-face.

"Look at you," she said, scanning me up and down.

I didn't even hear Emily come in behind me. In her bouncy voice she said to my parents, "Hello! How can I help you?"

"You can help me by letting us take our son home. Come on, James!" Mom grabbed my arm and began to make her way to the door.

"James is free to leave whenever he wants to. Of course, we'd have to remove the portal and he wouldn't get his money..."

Mom stopped stiff.

"Portal?" Dad asked.

I shook Mom off me. "The hell do you care what I'm doing?"

"James, don't talk to your mother like that." Dad spoke slightly above an indoor voice.

Mom glared at Emily. "You can't do this, you bubble-headed bitch."

Emily's broad grin demoted to a half smirk. Her voice deepened again. "James signed all the contracts. Whatever happens is in his hands."

Emily looked to me and her voice bubbled up quite suddenly, "What do you say, James?"

I stared straight into Mom's eyes, wide and glistening with hurt. "I'm not going anywhere."

"There you have it!" Emily smiled at my parents. "Shall I show you out or will we need to get the authorities involved?"

Mom gazed at me, unbelieving. Her eyes started to water even more. Dad gently put his hands on her shoulder and turned her around. As they went outside, Mom dropped her head and began to cry. The portal gave off a soothing hum, but my heart dropped.

Emily put her hand on my shoulder and beamed proudly. "See how much control you've taken over your life?"

For the rest of that day I stayed in bed thinking about what happened that morning. I hadn't seen Mom cry since Grandma died. I then thought about how much Mom would cry if I were to die. But I wasn't dying, was I?

I'm underweight, I look like death, the portal in my stomach is sucking me dry, and not only will no one around me stop it, they condone it. I do, too. How the hell do I get out of this?

Maybe I was selfish. But it was Delambre and Emily who were exploiting the sad and insecure. To them I was just step one in a

46

production line. Crank the machine to max efficiency until it breaks, because when it does there are plenty of others.

If I died Dad would be devastated and Mom would never be the same. Brandon would no longer have anyone who foolishly loves the Chiefs as much as him.

This wasn't just about my weight, I realized. This was about my life: not just mine but the lives of those who care about me. I needed to end this. I needed to get this damn thing out of me.

I drifted to sleep. The next morning I marched toward Emily's office.

The building was livelier than I'd ever seen before. On the far other end of the hall, I could see staff in white coats slipping in and out of rooms. A staff member came toward me holding a tray with fruit, bacon and waffles on it. I thought it was for me, and wondered why they would be bringing me food. But she opened the door to another bedroom. Inside, I could see a thin young woman sitting at her bed. When she made eye contact with me, the woman looked surprised and uncomfortable. The staff member turned and shut the door.

Emily was hanging her coat up when I entered and slammed the door shut. Her warm smile seemed to mock my anger.

"Good..."

"I want it out. I don't want to do this anymore."

"Haven't we had this discussion before?" She sighed and approached me. "Get some breakfast, then we'll talk some more."

"No, I've made my decision."

Emily put her hands on my shoulders, squeezing a bit. "You know what I've read? Very interesting. Some people are doomed to always be overweight. They can exercise and eat healthy as much as possible, but the weight will always come back!"

I ripped myself away from her, "You can't do this to people!"

Her tone lowered, "Do what? I'm not forcing you to stay here, it's all up to you. I'm just saying, you've made so much progress."

I lifted my shirt to show her my ribs, "Look at me!"

"You signed the contracts. You understood the risks. How much weight you gain or lose is in your control."

I lowered my shirt again and shook my head. "Get this out of me!"

"If you get that removed, you'll never have control of your weight again. For the rest of your life you'll..."

The portal gave a hum that made me so queasy, I felt dizzy. I had to stop her before she could convince me again. I snatched a "Delambre" pen from the holder on her desk and jammed it into her muscular right leg. She screamed in pain and dropped to her knee.

"You bastard!" She shrieked at me like a banshee.

I grabbed another pen and pointed it at her face threateningly, I couldn't keep myself from trembling.

Emily glared at me. "Fine," she snarled. "I hope you get big and fat!"

I woke up in front of the great big gun. The procedure was over. I half expected a hum, but there was none. To my left stood Emily, leaning away from her wounded and bandaged leg, with two staff members. To my right were two police officers.

As they escorted me out of the building, my hands cuffed behind my back, my thoughts raced.

Am I doing the right thing? Did I just overreact? Am I selfish with no regard for the greater good? Is Delambre right? Or should Emily be in cuffs too? Maybe all that "feeding the world" stuff was bullshit. After all, "cheap" doesn't mean "free".

Have I doomed myself?

When we came into the reception area, I was surprised to find it filled with five people: four women and one man, heads down, signing the deadly contracts. They all looked normal weight, healthy. They looked up at me. I recognized the look in their eyes: fear, no confidence, and shame.

I shouted at them. I told them not to do this, to leave. As much as I resisted, the police pulled me out the door with ease. I continued to shout at the terrified people, leaping and kicking into the air. The police were practically carrying me by my arms at this point.

I never felt lighter in my life.

Anthony Engebretson is a Nebraska-based writer, cat lover and recovering pessimist. He writes short film scripts, short stories and novels.

You can read more about him in his blog at:
https://raccoonalleyblog.wordpress.com

Look for the Union Label
By Desmond Warzel

"Where to, mac?"

If not for the silence of the taxi's electric engine, the threefold anachronism of a cabbie who 1) greeted his passengers verbally instead of grunting or scowling, 2) did so in English, and 3) possessed a genuine New York accent, might almost have convinced Maldonado that it was 1965 instead of 2065.

"Forty-fourth, between Seventh and Eighth," said Maldonado. "The Helen Hayes Theater."

"I thought it was the Planned Parenthood Theater now," said the cabbie as he activated the meter and eased the car into traffic.

"It was. Then it was the Al Jazeera Theater, then the Fox News Theater, then the Chico's Bail Bonds Theater, then the Monsanto Theater. Now it's the Helen Hayes again."

"Probably for the best."

"Say, can I trouble you for a receipt when we get there? This is a business expense."

"Sure thing, mac. What line of work you in? Acting?"

"Android repair."

"You putting me on? Can't believe there's much call for it these days."

"In a city of ten million, there's just enough business to keep one guy afloat. Kind of like typewriter repair."

The cabbie's genial laugh was cut short as he spiked the brakes to avoid rear ending the car ahead. Traffic had suddenly become paralyzed in all directions.

"This construction never ends. They do the same work over and over and hope we won't notice. Lousy unions are killing this city."

Maldonado made a noncommittal noise.

"Android repair. No kidding. Well, you live here long enough, you see one or two of everything, I suppose."

To get an honest-to-goodness science-fiction-type robot, you must do two things: build a machine that mimics natural movement, and

53

design a processor that simulates intelligent thought.

The former task had been all but conquered, and robots of various configurations now traversed all manner of deadly terrain in the name of exploration or exploitation. Artificial intelligence had proved uncrackable, however, so such machines had only a rudimentary logic to assist them in their programmed tasks.

Likewise, the realistic humanoid robots that followed. Most of these had ended up in show business, on the assumption that a handsome, brainless shell into which scripts were fed would seem right at home among actors.

The logic was sound, but nobody cared. An android could be programmed to play Richard III in the style of Olivier, but to audiences, it was nothing they hadn't already seen in the Hall of Presidents at Disney World. The fad had passed, but not before almost every theater and acting troupe had acquired at least one robot, which was now too out-of-demand to sell and too valuable to junk.

What's the difference between an android and a washed-up actor? One of them has an <u>excuse</u> for its inability to perceive its own obsolescence.

"Helen Hayes," announced the cabbie. He named an ungodly sum, which Maldonado paid in cash. "Think I'd live closer to the Theater District if I did most of my business there," he continued, handing over a receipt.

"Take a look at my bank statement sometime. That should solve the riddle." Maldonado handed the driver several more bills. "You can bet nobody will be tipping <u>me</u> today."

He introduced himself to the young man waiting in the lobby. "Garrett Maldonado, Greased Lightning Android Repair."

They shook hands. "Jody Gill of the Planned Parenthood Players. The city keeps losing our name-change paperwork."

"I guess revivals of <u>Baby</u>, <u>Cry-Baby</u>, and <u>Hallelujah, Baby</u> are out of the question just now."

"The robot's onstage. Follow me."

The stage was bare except for some painted crates standing in for furniture. The android stood at the center, dressed in simple black, one arm extended in mid-gesture. It was handsome, blonde, seemingly Northern European. They'd named it Keanu, after one of the great turn-of-the-century actors.

"We use it for practicing our lines." said Jody. "The union doesn't like us to do that with another actor."

"The same way baseball pitchers won't help out with batting practice."

"Right. Sometimes we'll stick it in a crowd scene. No speaking parts; the union looks askance. Or we'll put it in the chorus and run a little prize drawing among those audience members who correctly identify it."

"Whatever puts butts in seats, I suppose."

"I was doing some improv with it and it just shut down."

"Improv?"

"A little bit here and there keeps the mind sharp."

"I've never seen one capable of real improv."

"That's Keanu for you."

Maldonado set down his toolbox and circled Keanu appraisingly, searching in vain for obvious mechanical problems. Jody looked around for something useful to do, gave up, and took a seat on one of the crates.

"Might be a power issue." Maldonado tugged at the collar of Keanu's shirt, exposing a raised, flesh-colored circle the size of a standard piece of pepperoni. He swiveled it aside and poked about in the resultant opening, finally pulling out a length of electrical cord that unspooled continuously from inside the android's torso as Maldonado trod the boards looking for an outlet.

He'd finally discovered one behind the backdrop when there was a commotion backstage and a coverall-clad figure came running in, stage right.

"Darrell McKinney, International Brotherhood of Electrical Workers, Local Three. Just keep some daylight between those prongs and that outlet and there won't be any trouble. Otherwise, we'll lock this place up tight as a drum."

Maldonado declined to rise, instead pointing at the toolbox. "It's right inside the top tray."

McKinney grudgingly opened the box. When he saw Maldonado's IBEW card, his expression changed as if a switch had been flipped. "Carry on, brother," he said encouragingly, before flashing a vague gesture of solidarity--halfway between a fistbump attempt and a Black Power salute--and sauntering offstage.

Once Keanu was plugged in, all the indicator lights beneath its synthetic flesh came up green. Power was no problem.

"Might be the servomotors," Maldonado mused.

He'd no sooner opened the tiny access panels at Keanu's elbows and shoulders when a voice came from over his shoulder.

"Sheila Alvarez, International Association of Machinists and Aerospace Workers, Local Four Forty-Seven. Lay one finger on that servomotor and everybody walks."

"My IAM card's in the box."

"Carry on, brother."

"Any chance I could trouble you for the loan of a screwdriver, <u>brother</u>?"

Keanu's servomotors were fine above the waist. Its hips and knees were the more likely culprits anyway.

For Maldonado, pushing forty from the wrong side, prolonged squatting wasn't an option. He went to retrieve one of the painted crates to serve as a chair.

"Emilio Frank, International Alliance of Theatrical Stage Employees, Local One. Drop that crate, or it'll be six months before another prop gets moved in this town."

Maldonado actually did drop it. This one had taken even him by surprise, and he had to dig deep in the box to find his IATSE card.

"Lila Fletcher, Theatrical Wardrobe Union, Local Seven Sixty-Four. Don't even think about taking that robot's pants down."

"Card's in the toolbox. You find it."

Keanu's lower servos checked out as well. "And that wouldn't make it stop talking, anyway," muttered Maldonado. "Come on, think." It was obviously something in the processor, but he hated taking android brains apart. He could never get them reassembled without a few minuscule pieces left over, even if the androids never seemed to notice. He glanced at Jody Gill, who had been regarding the proceedings from her seat upstage. "You say you were doing improv? What, exactly?"

"A science fiction parody."

"How original."

"I started the skit as West Side Story; it was Keanu who decided spaceships were landing at Lincoln Center. I just went along."

"The android decided?"

"Keanu is very proactive. Anyway, before I knew it, we were on the Enterprise. I was the

captain, Keanu was an android who had
infiltrated my crew..."

"So you had a robot, whose sole function is
to imitate human behavior, playing the part of a
robot trying to imitate human behavior. No
wonder it shut down; you probably fried what
little logic it possessed. I'm surprised you didn't
order it to define love, or come up with a rhyme
for 'orange.'"

"Both, actually," said Jody.

"You're kidding."

"I like classic <u>Trek</u>. What do you want
from me?"

Maldonado had stopped listening. "Maybe
we can do this without messing around in its
skull," he mused.

"How?"

"The same way you help any actor who's
frozen up. Feed him the next line."

It had cost him an hour of fretting and
strutting upon the stage, but Maldonado devised
an elegant solution to the robot's quandary--a
fourteen-line sonnet defining love, with three

distinct rhymes for "orange"--which he now entered manually via the miniature data pad in the small of Keanu's back.

(Alas, he failed to write it down, so the poem's text is lost to history.)

Keanu jolted to life and recited the sonnet as if Jody Gill's character had only just given the order.

"I'll be damned," said Jody. "You did it."

"Okay, Jody; have at it."

"Have at what?"

"It might get hung up again if it doesn't return to its starting state."

"What do I do?"

"Act, boy!"

"What should I say?"

"Never mind." Maldonado took a deep breath, paused to clear his head, and slipped into the role of the Enterprise captain. "Very well, robot," he said haltingly. "You've defeated my riddles. Now what the hell are you doing aboard my ship?"

"My mission is more important than your inferior brain can comprehend," said Keanu, and the improv skit was off and running.

Somehow the <u>Enterprise</u> crash-landed in the Emerald City, where hilarity ensued.

This led to a peace negotiation with the Smurfs done entirely in <u>Monty Python</u> quotes (miraculously, without the words "lumberjack," "parrot," or "inquisition" appearing even once).

Amazingly, this became a reimagining of <u>Breakfast at Tiffany's</u> with the sexes reversed and the happy ending excised (thus allowing the story to make sense for once).

As improbable scenario after improbable scenario unfurled, linked by the most tenuous of connections, spurred on by Keanu's impossible creativity, with Maldonado barely managing to keep up, until it came full circle to the alien invasion of Lincoln Center, only this time <u>they</u> were the invaders, and they gained a new respect for humanity as they watched Riff of the Jets and Bernardo of the Sharks put aside their differences and give their lives in defense of the Upper West Side.

It all made sense at the time.

When it was over, Maldonado was sweating, breathing heavily, looking Keanu right in the eyes. They flickered with light and life and awareness; with fear that this new conception of itself was only temporary. The robot dared not speak out of turn, but its eyes beseeched Maldonado to keep the skit going.

Then came the nearly-imperceptible sound of logic pathways slamming home into their proper configurations, and Keanu snapped to attention and stood awaiting its next command. The flicker in its eyes departed.

There was, for a minute, silence.

And then, from the back of the room: "Shawn Gibbs, Actors' Equity Association. You're in big trouble, buddy." The voice carried well; the Helen Hayes Theater was small by Broadway standards.

"You're a little late to the party, Gibbs," retorted Jody.

"It's all this construction," said Gibbs. "These unions are crippling this town."

Maldonado collected his toolbox and hopped down from the stage. He flashed his Equity card in Gibbs's face. "Can you just pay me, please?" he asked wearily. "I want to leave before the Dramatist's Guild finds out I composed original material."

He caught a cab immediately outside the theater. It was the same driver. It happens.

"Back to the office, mac?"

"You got it."

"Get everything squared away?"

"If the check clears, I might almost break even." They rode uptown in silence. The traffic had thinned out a little.

"Something on your mind, mac?"

"May I ask you a question? With your assurance that it doesn't leave this cab?"

"Think of me as a priest. Or a bartender."

"Suppose you had just witnessed the spontaneous generation of artificial intelligence in an android. Would you tell anyone?"

"Sounds like a recipe for panic to me. I'd keep that under my hat."

"I thought so, too."

Several more minutes of silence went by. Maldonado stared into space. He looked up only when he felt the cab slowing to a stop in the middle of the block.

The cabbie's arms hung slack at his sides. "Both brachial servomotors at once. What are the odds? Well, if it had to happen, today's the day for it. Trouble you for a little mechanical assistance here, mac?"

Something inside Maldonado wouldn't let him even pretend to be surprised. "Sorry," he said. "I'm not carrying any tools. This box is all union cards."

"No problem." Steering with his knees, the cabbie maneuvered the car jerkily toward the curb. "Would you mind calling the dispatcher for me?"

This was a brighter and more interesting ending to the workday than Maldonado had even considered hoping for. "I'll do you one better.

Move over and I'll drive you back myself. We can chat on the way. Maybe stop at my office; I'd like to have a look at you."

"Can't let you do it, mac." Maldonado slumped against the window and watched the cars pass by, barely listening to the incapacitated cabbie. "National Taxi Workers' Alliance would skin me alive. Not to mention bringing this city to a standstill. I tell you, if it's not one thing with these unions, it's another..."

Desmond Warzel is the author of a few dozen short stories in the science fiction, fantasy, and horror genres. Many of these are humorous; occasionally, this is intentional. He lives and writes in northwestern Pennsylvania. His blog, the infrequently-updated *Jobless Insomniacs Motorcycle Club*, can be found at http://desmondwarzel.wordpress.com

The Radium Room
by Tony Conaway

I sat alone in what used to be a boiler room underneath a tenement building on 81st Street. The tenement is long gone, and this underground room was forgotten when the fancy new apartment building was built on this site.

I was looking at some new material for the upcoming elections in Local 147. My union. The Sandhogs. If it has to do with something underneath street level in New York City, the Sandhogs are probably involved. We dig the tunnels, the subways, even – sometimes - the foundations for the buildings.

But I'm the only member of the Sandhogs Union who actually lives underground. Me, Jake Rosenthal. That's because I'm the troubleshooter, and I've made plenty of enemies in the 33 years I've been doing this thing.

Some of my enemies are human. Most of them are guys who tried to run drug labs underground.

Some of my enemies aren't human.

You see, I'm the guy who knows about the tunnels under Manhattan. I don't know it all – no one does. For over 200 years, people have been digging tunnels and subways and sewers under the city. If there ever were records of where all those tunnels were, they've been lost.

And some of the tunnels weren't dug by human hands.

I'm not talking about machine-dug tunnels, either. There are things down here you don't want to know about.

Some of those tunnels move. Yes, they move. Some aren't fixed in space. Some aren't fixed in time.

But when something comes out of those tunnels and causes trouble for the people above, the City asks me to fix it. They even pay me.

I was reading negative ads on fliers put out by the two opposing candidates for president of my union. Or at least pretending to. Whoever won, it wouldn't have any effect on what I do.

That's when a pneumatic tube went <u>shunk</u>, and a note came down to my boiler room. I stood, fetched the message, and read it. The pneumatic tube was the way people communicated with me. There's no mail delivery down here. No cell phone or wi-fi coverage, either.

Once again, I was needed.

I put my shoes on and started to make the long trip down to 1 Police Plaza.

I'd been summoned by a member of the NYPD. This was not unusual. What was different was that the officer who requested my assistance was with the Terrorism Squad.

You might expect a cop who spent most days listening to wiretaps of suspected terrorists to be out of shape. But Detective Cesar Loperfido was one of those cops who went to the gym instead of the bar after work. He was built like a wedge, with the sort of muscles that can tear phone books in half (if anyone used phone books anymore).

He was listening to a recorded wiretap when a uniform brought me to his desk. I waited. Even though Loperfido had earphones on, I could hear just enough to identify the language of the wiretap. The uniform dutifully waited next to me until Loperfido waved her off. He eyed the police day pass that hung around my neck, as well as the one from the City of New York identifying me as a "consultant."

Finally, the call was over. He stood up and looked me in the eye, which is more than some cops bother to do.

"You're the consultant about what's below the sidewalks?"

"Jake Rosenthal." He said his name and we shook hands. Then he pulled a chair over so I could sit next to his desk. We sat.

"Where did you learn Arabic?" I asked. I was guessing Monterrey, where the US Military trains soldiers in foreign languages. Loperfido had the look of an ex-soldier.

"You recognized that as Arabic?" Typical cop, answering a question with a question.

I shrugged. "I'm a Jew. I've made a few trips to Israel. Arabic is surprisingly close to Hebrew. I'm not fluent in either, but I get by."

"Uh-huh. Well, my mother was from Malta. She taught me her language. Maltese is actually a variant of Arabic, even though it's written using the Roman alphabet, not Arabic script. So I was halfway to being an Arabic speaker when the Army decided I'd make a good intelligence officer and sent me to Arabic class."

It was time to get down to business. "So what can I help you with, Detective?"

He pulled a file out of his desk drawer, but didn't open it.

"Ever since 9-11, we've had different types of sensors operating around New York City. Some try to detect high concentrations of poisons or diseases that might be released by terrorists. Others detect radiation."

And how many of these work correctly? I wanted to ask. I didn't, though.

"Unfortunately," he continued, "there are other sources of radiation beside terrorist devices. For instance, people undergo radiation treatment for cancer. These people set off our radiation detectors all the time. Once, we called out a SWAT team for what turned out to be four cancer patients in a car, coming back from a self-help meeting for the terminally ill."

He paused, as if he was remembering something that went very wrong. So I jumped in. "There are also hot spots of radiation all over the place," I said.

"Right! Exactly!" the Detective said. "You might think that we've found all the radioactive hot spots around the five boroughs. You'd be wrong. In the first half of the 20th century, there were so many laboratories and industries using radioactive materials that we don't have a record of them all."

He went on. "I mean, frigging *shoe stores* had X-ray machines! They X-rayed your feet for what they claimed was a better fit. No one knew how dangerous radioactivity was!"

"Well," I said, "if you think New York has a lot of hot spots, try walking around Moscow with a Geiger counter. *If they'd let you, which they don't.* The results will make you book the next flight out of Russia."

He didn't seem to hear me. Instead, he opened the file and put a photo on the desk. It showed a sickly-looking young man in a hospital bed. He was balding, but the hair he had left was very long. And his jaw was wired shut, the way they do when it's broken.

"This vagrant set off the radiation meters. I happened to be nearby, going home, so I was the arresting officer. He was disoriented and resisted arrest. I slammed him against a building while trying to cuff him. He apparently hit his face against the wall, and his jaw shattered. That was a surprise, because I didn't think he hit that hard."

He tapped at the photo. "He was taken to Bellevue. He had some priors for drug possession, so he was identified from his fingerprints as one Harold Duane Van Scoyk. Variously known as 'Harry,' 'Hairy Harry,' or 'Harry the Hippie.' But here's the thing: those arrests were back in 1968, at which time he was identified as 28 years old. Does that look like a 75-year-old to you?"

"Nope," I said. "He doesn't look healthy, but he looks no older than 35. Maybe 40, tops."

"Agreed. Harry didn't tell us his name – or anything, for that matter – because he was delirious. He died three days later. Cause of death was ruled to be radiation poisoning. The autopsy shows that his jaw was riddled with radiation, which is why it was so brittle."

"So he'd been eating something radioactive," I said.

This time I'd surprised him. "How do you know eating radioactive material makes your jaw brittle?"

I sighed. "Look up 'Radium Girls' on the internet. They were employees of companies that manufactured watch dials with glow-in-the-dark numbers. They glowed because they were painted on using radium paint."

"Here's the really nasty part: those poor women who painted the dials were trained to get a tight point on their brushes by licking them. They actually put the tip of their paintbrushes in their mouths. In the process, they swallowed a tiny bit of radium paint – day in, day out. Month in, month out. Some of them did it for years. So we know what swallowing radioactive material does to your jaw and bones."

"Huh," the Detective said. "Well, we can't close this case until we pinpoint where Harry got exposed. From his record and from asking around, I found out that Harry used to sell psychedelic mushrooms in the East Village. This was back in the late 60's and early 70's. He disappeared about 1974. People knew where he hung out, but no one seemed to know where he lived. Our assumption is that grew his mushrooms in a basement somewhere in or near the Village, and that basement is contaminated with radiation."

"Just so I understand," I said, "you want me to find that radioactive basement. You don't need me to explain how Harry stopped aging in 1974."

"Right," said Loperfido. "However he did it, I doubt anyone would believe it. And I'm with the Terrorism Squad. I just need to find that radioactive hot spot, so no terrorist can collect the stuff and use it as a dirty bomb."

"Ok. Let me show you how you have to type up the requisition to hire me. If it's not done right, I don't get paid. I'll also need to borrow some equipment."

###

How Harry showed up in the present while still a young man – albeit dying from radiation -- may have been a mystery to the NYPD. But they didn't know about the tunnels that are unstuck in time and space. I figured that Harry somehow found one, and in his delirium, wandered through. From 1974 to the present day in a few easy, terrifying steps.

Part of my job as the one-and-only underground specialist was to seal off those tunnels. Whenever I found one, Local 147 loaned me some men and material, and they built a wall to block the tunnel. No questions asked.

But these tunnels kept moving, so it was a never-ending process. I don't know who built these tunnels -- I just know a little about how they work. I also don't know if anyone can change history by going through to the past. But I – and my predecessors in this job – didn't want to take that chance, so we seal the tunnels off.

When I was a kid growing up in the city, I had an uncle who kept homing pigeons on the roof of his apartment building. Homing pigeons wouldn't be much use underground, so I developed something new: homing rats.

77

These were ordinary Norway rats, just like the millions that infest every city on earth. I bred them in clean cages, since I didn't want to catch anything from them. Rats not only carry fleas, but they can spread disease though their urine. I knew a Sandhog who caught Korean hemorrhagic fever from rodent urine; it nearly killed him.

To make them *homing* rats, I feed them an addictive substance. No, I won't tell you what it is. But my junkie rats all want to come back to me to get their fix.

Detective Loperfido gave me with a supply of two different types of dosimeters. These are cheap, one-use radiation detectors. Once they detect dangerous levels of radiation, the color changes on a display. It stays that way, so you have to use a new one each time – assuming the person using it hasn't died. Loperfido gave me two different types. One was a little box that you could pin to your lapel. The other was on a zip-tie that you put around your wrist. I'd never put them on my homing rats before, so I tried both. I put the zip-tie around the body of some rats. The box type I just super-glued to the backs of some shaved rats, which is how scientists attach tracking devices or other instruments to rats. That process got me bitten a few times. I also sprayed each rat with some glow-in-the-dark paint, to make it easier to see the vicious little bastards.

Then I took the rats to the entrances to the Lower Manhattan tunnels. A few minutes with a crowbar opened the walls that concealed each tunnel –- I would get the Sandhogs to wall them over again when I was done. I put two caged rats at the mouth of each tunnel. Then I played a recording of loud carnivore noises at the same time I opened the cages. The startled rats ran away from the noise, down the tunnels.

And I waited.

These tunnels may move between time and space, but they look pretty much like ordinary tunnels. No special effects, no glowing lights.

Sitting there, waiting, at the mouth of a tunnel, my mind wandered. I was getting old. I had to pass on all the knowledge I'd acquired, but I hadn't found anyone willing to replace me. The work was too dangerous, too lonely, too creepy. I'd tried nine apprentices so far, and each one eventually quit. Or died.

After about twenty minutes, I took out some of my special rat food with its addictive secret sauce. I put it atop a small Coleman camp stove and lit the flame. Heated, the food had quite an aroma. Just to make sure my rats could smell it at the other end, I took a small, battery-powered fan and blew the aroma down the tunnel.

A few minutes later, at least one of my homing rats was home. But in the first two tunnels, the dosimeters remained clear.

On the third tunnel, both rats came back. The one with the zip-tie dosimeter had apparently chewed the band off. But the other still had his super-glued dosimeter, and it was in the red. I'd found the tunnel that led to a radioactive hot spot.

That didn't prove that this was the hot spot I was looking for. I would have to go through the tunnel myself to ascertain that.

Fortunately, the dosimeter indicated that the radiation dosage was within the safe range. Wherever the tunnel went, it wasn't to the inside of a nuclear reactor.

I sighed and looked at my homing rats. "I'm too old for this," I told them.

Then I euthanized each one with a quick injection. My rat stock was clean, but those two had likely picked up fleas (and, possibly, a disease or two) on their travels. I couldn't risk putting them back in with the rest of my stock and infecting them. And if I released them, they would still try to get back to the others to get the drug-infused chow that they were addicted to.

"Like the man says, 'you can't go home again,'" I told the corpses of my two little junkies.

I stood at the entrance of the tunnel, debating whether or not to do this now, or put it off until tomorrow. The only thing that made sense was to do it now. These tunnels moved, and you never knew when it would happen. If I waited until tomorrow, I might have to search for this tunnel all over again.

I'd been crouching next to my rat cage. My knees made noise when I stood up. When had that started? Ten years ago? Twenty?

There was no guarantee that I would be able to come back. I recalled that I used to say a prayer and leave a last letter for my people before I went down one of these tunnels.

But I hadn't prayed in years. And I didn't have any people, not any more.

Instead, I misquoted Shakespeare: *If t'were done, t'were best done quickly.* Lady McBeth's version was longer and more convoluted.

Then I made my way down the tunnel.

Since I knew that I'd probably have to traverse one of these tunnels, I'd prepared. I was searching for the site of radiation, and radiation was not even discovered until 1896, by a Frenchman. The sort of commercial usage of radiation I was looking for hadn't begun in New York until after 1910. So I was carrying coins and currency from a hundred years ago. I was wearing overalls, a long-sleeve wool shirt, a light jacket, and a cloth cap. No zippers or Velcro; just buttons. This outfit was marvelously timeless, and warm enough for anything except the dead of winter. It was the uniform of a laborer...and that's essentially what I was. A laborer with a very bizzare specialty.

Before the mouth of the tunnel was out of sight, I looked back. Although it felt as if I'd been walking in a straight line, the floor I'd just left appeared to tilt at a 90 degree angle. I have no idea if gravity was skewed inside these tunnels, or if it was just some sort of optical effect. As I said, these tunnels didn't come with an instruction manual. All I knew came from my own experience and the advice of my predecessor, a man named Arkady Belnikoff. He told me that the there was a sort of synchronicity about the tunnels. There was even a theory about it, something called the Novikov self-consistency principle. Don't ask me to explain it. All I know is that time-travel seems to bring you to something important. In this case, I hoped it was the location of the radiation.

As always, the end of the tunnel came up unexpectedly. There was no hiding inside the mouth and poking your head out to look around. One moment you were approaching the mouth; the next, you were outside the tunnel. It was as if it spat you out, although there was no sensation of being pushed. Perhaps a better way to describe is this: it's as if the tunnel mouth was a carpet, and someone pulled it out from under you.

So I stumbled into the past, into a cold, dark room. The only light seemed to come from a square in the ceiling above.

I took out a flashlight but didn't turn it on. The LED bulbs would illuminate the entire room, but it would also ruin my night vision. Instead, I let my eyes adjust to the darkness. In less than a minute, I could see that I was in an unfinished, dirt-floor basement. The ceiling was wood – I could see some light between slats of floorboard. The square of light was some sort of trap door. And I could hear voices from above me, all female.

There was also the scritch of a boom on the floor above. Someone was sweeping up. They swept dust and some small bits of trash into the trap door, and the dust filtered down into the basement.

And it glowed.

I looked at the floor. There were little glowing spots of light all over it.

I pulled out my radiation meter, which was a more complex version of the dosimeter. It even had an illuminated control panel. And it said that this room was radioactive. I wasn't in immediate danger, but I wanted to get out of this basement. I really didn't want to breathe in that radioactive dust.

I'd found the probable source of Harry's radioactivity. But I needed to know exactly where this room was. I didn't have a GPS beacon with a hundred-year battery to leave here. And, even if I had one (did they make such things?), someone might steal it. I needed the street address of this building.

I pulled my scarf up, covering my mouth and nose. Breathing though it might afford me some protection.

From upstairs, a bell rang. Then a loud male voice shouted, "That's it for today, girls. Be sure to clean your tools before you put them away. Sophie, I have to go. Lock up for me." A female voice responded, and the sounds of at least a dozen workers preparing to leave. The trap door slammed shut, leaving the glowing dots the only source of illumination.

It was time to get a clearer picture of the basement. I turned my flashlight on low. There were no mushrooms, but I'd traveled in time. I might be here years before Harry started growing mushrooms here. I saw some pipes, one of which smelled like the building's main connection to the sewers. There was the building's old boiler, no longer in use. Evidently, this building was now heated through a connection to a local steam plant. I saw a boarded-up space that was probably the coal chute for the old boiler. The boards were heavy. There was little chance I could remove them to exit the basement, not without being noticed.

Fortunately, I found a stairwell in one dark corner. With the coal chute blocked, the stairs seemed to be the only exit – unless I wanted to go back through the tunnel.

I made my way up the basement stairs.

There was a stout wooden door at the top of the stairs, locked. I searched my pockets for my lock picks. I was no expert locksmith, but I didn't expect a simple lock – possibly made before I was born – to give me much trouble.

Except my lock picks weren't there. I'd forgotten them.

The mighty time-traveling troubleshooter had left his tools behind! I remembered putting my lock pick case on my desk as I dressed this morning. It was probably still there.

Could I break this door down? Rapping it, I could tell it was a solid slab of wood, not some modern hollow-core door. And the stairwell landing was narrow. There was no room to get any momentum, even if I could break it down.

So I did the only thing I could think of: I pushed down my scarf to uncover my mouth, then I pounded on the door and yelled, "Hey! You locked me in!"

After a minute of pounding, a female voice called out, "Who's down there?"

I was dressed as a laborer, but there wasn't much in the basement to pretend to be working on. The stench of the sewage line gave me an idea. "The plumber!" I shouted back. "I was working on the pipes, and someone locked me in!"

"Just a minute," the female voice said. I heard several keys being tried in the lock. On the fourth try, the lock turned and the door opened.

I stepped into a none-too-wide hallway. The best defense was a good offence, so I pretended to be angry. "Didn't you know I was down there?"

I didn't get a look at her until I closed the door behind me. She was dressed like a working class woman in cold weather, so it was hard to place the time. I guessed this was between the wars – the 1920s or 1930s. She wore a work apron – splattered with glowing paint – over a fairly shapeless, long-sleeved, ankle-length dress. And she was not cowed by my feigned anger in the slightest.

"And how was I supposed to know you were down there?" she said. "I have enough to do with supervising a dozen lazy girls, without keeping track of what's going on elsewhere in the building!"

"Is there a problem, Sophie?" said a male voice.

We turned. A man in business dress was coming down a none-too-wide staircase from upstairs. The collar of his dress shirt was part of the shirt, not separate. Detachable celluloid collars for men went out of fashion after the First World War. He carried a heavy overcoat draped over one arm.

"It's just the plumber, Mr. Reading," she said.

"Plumber? Good." He looked at me. "The water pressure up on the third floor is abysmal. See if you can fix that."

He eased past us into a small foyer, then exited the building.

"Who hired you to work on the plumbing?" she asked me.

"Your landlord. The tenants have been complaining, as you can see."

"Huh," she said. "Well, I have to lock up. Are you done for the day?"

"No. I asked my brother to bring me the piping I needed, but he didn't make it back, yet."

"Well, it's not like there's anything to steal in the basement, so I suppose I can leave it unlocked. We lock the front door to the street after closing time, but if you stay in here, you can open it for your brother. Will that be all right?"

"Absolutely. Sorry to be such a bother." I gave her my best smile.

"The only bother will be if I've missed my bus. The next one won't be along for 20 minutes."

She took off her paint-stained apron, walked a few steps back to an open door, and went inside. She came out again a few seconds later, closed and locked the door. She'd exchanged the apron for a heavy wool coat, which she put on. It was only then that I noticed a sign above the door that read "Klopman's Watch Parts."

Hell and damnation! She was one of the Radium Girls!

"Goodnight, then," she said. She eased past me and went out the front door.

I was too stunned to say anything. The reason I knew about the Radium Girls is that my own grandmother was one of them. Sophia Pollock was her name. They called her *Sophie*. And the businessman from upstairs had called this woman "Sophie!"

I had to warn her about the dangers of the radium paint she worked with!

I ran to the front door and opened it. I didn't see her anywhere. I wanted to run out and find her, but the door would lock behind me.

I fumbled through my pockets and pulled out a small roll of duct tape. Never leave home without it – at least not in my profession. I used it to tape the lock open so it wouldn't lock me out.

Then I was out in the street, looking up and down for her. Again, there was no sign of her, but I saw a bus several blocks away. I took a second to glance at the building I'd just exited and memorized the address. Then I took off after the bus.

It was snowing, and my light jacket was nowhere near warm enough. But the exertion of running kept me reasonably warm.

I'd gone only half a block when I happened to glance in the large front window of a coffee shop. There she was, calmly sipping from a cup at a table near the window!

I skidded to a stop on the snow-slick sidewalk. OK, I found her. But what do I say? I walked under a canopy to get out of the snow, and tried to remember everything I'd heard about my grandmother. I'd never met her – she'd died of cancer many years before I was born.

She'd filed a lawsuit against her employer before she died, but the company took almost a decade to settle. Sophie was long gone by then. My mother said that Sophie's settlement got the family through the Great Depression.

I looked though the window of the store behind me. It was a stationery store, and had several calendars on display. Apparently, this was February of 1924.

OK. Mother told me that Sophie went to work after her husband died during the Spanish Flu Pandemic, which followed World War One. Mother was Sophie's only child – her husband died before they could have another. And she said that Sophie died just before the Great Depression started, after two years of being deathly ill. The Depression started in 1929, so Sophie became ill around 1927.

Since this was 1924, Sophie was still healthy. Why would she believe me if I told her that radium would kill her?

Maybe it wasn't too late, if I could convince her to stop. I knew I had to try, even if it meant changing the past. My past, her future.

So I dusted the snow off my clothes and went into the coffee shop. Half the men inside seemed to be smoking – cigars, pipes, and the newly-popular cigarettes. I wondered if it was still considered scandalous for women to smoke in public. I suppressed an urge to cough from the smoke.

It was dinnertime, so there weren't any empty tables. Good – that gave me a plausible excuse to sit with Sophie.

"Hello again, Miss Sophie. There doesn't seem to be any free tables. May I join you?"

"I don't recall telling you my name, Mister?"

"Rosenthal. Jake Rosenthal, of Rosenthal and Sons Plumbing. And that fella from upstairs said your name as he was leaving."

"Oh, yes. Mr. Reading. Well, sit down."

I sat.

She looked a bit confused. "Did you lock yourself out of the building, Mr. Rosenthal? I can let you back in, but I'm only here because I missed my bus and it's too cold to wait outside."

"Thank you, Miss Sophie. My brother finally showed up. The *dreykop* got lost coming back, so I'm letting him carry our equipment down to the basement. I'm taking a short break while he contemplates the foolishness of not writing down the address of a job site."

"You're the older brother, I take it?"

"That I am, Miss Sophie. Although my brother can be such a *schlemiel* that I don't like to admit we're related." I was throwing in Yiddish words to try and bond with her, but she didn't seem to be impressed.

"Well, we can't pick our relatives. And it's Mrs., not Miss. Mrs. Pollock."

"Ah. Well, may I say that Mister Pollock is a very lucky man." Was I actually flirting with my own grandmother?

"He was, until the Great Flu took him."

"I'm sorry."

She shrugged. At that point a waitress asked what I'd like. I ordered coffee, and asked my grandmother if she'd like another tea or something to eat.

"Thank you, no. The next bus will be here shortly. My daughter and I live with my parents now, and I'll have dinner with them when I get home."

"A daughter. That's nice."

"She's a little *lapitut,* but I love her."

Demon wasn't a word I associated with my mother. But do we ever really know someone? And she was only about eight years old at the present.

Enough. Sophie's bus would be here soon. It was time to try and save her.

"Can I ask, what do you do at the watch company?"

"I paint watch faces all day. It's not exciting, but I'm glad for the work. Since the men came back from the War, there aren't as many jobs for women. But this is delicate work, and the watch companies think that women handle jobs that take a delicate touch better than men. Oh, and the owner made me supervisor over the girls. All that means is I get a set of keys and an extra 8 cents an hour."

"I saw glowing dust in the basement. Is that the paint?"

"Yes. That's dust from the radium paint. Another legacy of the war. The men in the trenches didn't always have a hand free to take out a pocket watch, so they started wearing watches around their wrists. And the trenches were dark, but radium paint on the dial let them see the time." She took a sip of her tea. "You weren't in the War, were you?"

My mind raced, counting the years against my age. "No, I wasn't. Too old. I suppose I could've volunteered back in the Spanish-American War, but I couldn't see myself as one of Teddy Roosevelt's Rough Riders."

She laughed, but she didn't make a joke about Jews not having any knack for horses or guns, like someone from my time might have. In this era, everyone my age had used horses. Automobiles only became popular after the War.

And plenty of rural people – including Jews -- used guns to hunt for food or to keep foxes away from their chickens.

"What does a radium watch look like? Do you wear one?" She was wearing her outercoat indoors, so she might have had a wristwatch under her sleeves.

"Me? No. We don't make women's watches with radium dials. And I have other things to spend my money on. But I can show you some radium."

She put her hands around her mouth, like a megaphone. But instead of shouting, she smiled broadly.

And her teeth *glowed.*

Until now, her teeth hadn't shown when she talked, or even when she laughed. That's another family trait.

And the glow was faint. You didn't really notice it unless her mouth was in shadow.

"That's...something."

"Some of the girls paint their fingernails with radium paint, but my daughter loves it when my teeth glow."

I looked down and took a sip of a truly terrible cup of coffee. The waitress had gotten it out of a huge cylindrical urn the size of a small water heater; the coffee had probably been boiling in there since lunchtime. Coffee was another thing that had improved greatly in the past hundred-odd years.

I sighed. This wasn't my time. The coffee was bad and so was medical knowledge.

Sophie's teeth and jaw were already irradiated. Before she died of cancer, all her teeth would fall our and her jaw would break from the simple pressure of trying to chew. And it was too late to do anything about it.

"Are you sure that's...healthy? You must swallow radium when you do that."

"I suppose. But Mr. Klopman swears that radium is safe."

"Well," I said as I stood up. "I'm sure you know by now, Mrs. Pollock, that men are terrible liars."

"This I know, Mr. Rosenthal."

"Good. I have to get back to work. Let me pay for your tea." She didn't protest. This was an era where men paid, and held the door for ladies.

I waved to the waitress, who brought over a check for a big ten cents: five cents for a coffee, five cents for tea. I took out an old fifty-cent coin and gave it to her saying, "Keep the change." Might as well make someone happy, even if I couldn't save my grandmother.

I had my back to my grandmother, so she hadn't witnessed my act of largess. Just then I saw a bus pull up. "Is that your ride, Mrs. Pollock?"

"Yes! Got to go! Thank you for the tea."

She rushed out. The bus was disgorging passengers at a stop right in front, so she made it in time.

Then she was gone.

I trudged back through the snow. I was glad to be out of the smoke-filled luncheonette, even if I wasn't dressed warmly enough for the cold. The sun had set, but the streetlights gave enough light to avoid the piles of snow.

The front door of my destination was still unlocked. After double-checking to make sure I had the correct address for Detective Loperfido, I went inside. I remembered to remove the duct tape so that the door would lock behind me.

Movement caught my eye. I realized that there must still be someone in an upstairs office, because they had just sent some mail down a mail chute. The front of the chute was glass, and you could see mail being sent down from upper floors. It was easier for the Postman to collect all the mail for the building here in the lobby, rather than tromp up to each floor. He'd deliver the mail into mailboxes attached to the wall near the entrance.

Another anachronism, at least to me. In my time, the Post Office was sliding into irrelevance. Here, it was so important that there were two deliveries each weekday.

I still had almost fifty dollars in old bills on me. I thought about mailing that money to Sophie, or to my mother. I knew the address. After

Sophie died, her parents had raised my mother in a small house they owned. My mother had pointed it out to me several times.

But I didn't have a stamp, or even an envelope. And was it really possible to change time? In any significant way? I had overtipped a waitress, and bought my grandmother a cup of tea, but those weren't life-changing events. Fifty dollars was probably over a month's wage for Sophie, and that had the potential to change history. Didn't it?

I didn't know. All I knew is that I was tired, and wanted to go home. I went down into the basement and returned through the tunnel.

Thankfully, the tunnel had not shifted away from where I entered. My gear was still piled next to the entrance.

The bodies of my two dead homing rats were where I'd left them, but there was a live rat sniffing at the corpses. It eyed me but didn't run away.

"You can't save anyone, brother," I told the rat. "Don't even try."

The rat must have agreed, because he shook his head and scuttled off.

Wearily, I gathered up my gear and headed back to the boiler room I called home.

Tony Conaway has written and ghostwritten everything from blogs to books. He has co-written business books published by McGraw-Hill, Macmillan and Prentice Hall. He writes fiction in just about every genre except erotica and romance. But make him an offer – he'll do those, too.

He can be found on Twitter as *@TonyConaway* and on Facebook as *Author Tony Conaway.* He interviews other authors at *wayneaconaway.blogspot.com*

Deepest Blue
by Ewan R Chapman

He gave me a key.

It was over 4 years ago now, at a meeting I held in parliament. All he said was 'I'll tell you when and where to use it'. Although it sounds cryptic, I didn't think so at the time. Over the course of our meetings I'd come to admire the man, and had realised that to question him often led to me being red faced and apologetic. His genius is legendary, but his trustworthiness and humility are not traits you'll read about in Time magazine.

As I enter Blue Enterprise's London headquarters I'm directed through the large reception towards a small elevator tucked behind a security desk where an attendant meets me. After stepping into the elevator she asks "which floor, Consul?" I reach into the inside pocket of my coat and retrieve the small key, turning it over in my hand.

The attendant looks down at my hand and smiles, emitting a gentle laugh that is, somehow, both mocking and genuine. She raises her hand, gesturing to the bank of elevator buttons to my left, I can see that they number in the early hundreds arranged in four vertical rows, but I fail to see what she is gesturing for me to do.

"Here, Consul" she says, pointing at a small opening at the top of the bank of numbers. I reach up slowly and insert the key, turning it clockwise. There is a loud 'bong' and the elevator doors gently slide shut. My eyes are drawn up to the display where a flashing letter 'P' has appeared, puzzlingly this doesn't correspond to any of the floors on the list.

"I take it we're headed to the penthouse then," I say.

"Your deduction is correct, Consul. Mr Blue doesn't hand out these keys very frequently. Now I'm sure you can understand why." She replies.

I suddenly feel my ears pop, despite having felt no upward motion. The sensation is unsettling but I must admit, very impressive. We quickly reach the penthouse and the doors open to a small anteroom. I step out into the room and see James,

Damien Blue's assistant, standing by a large oak door.

"Evening, Consul," says James as the elevator doors close behind me.

"Evening, James. I believe Mr Blue is expecting me," I admire the perfectly pressed seams of his suit, exquisitely tailored. The shade of navy complements his pale complexion perfectly.

James moves to the door and places his hand on the ornate handle. "Do you play Chess, Consul?" he asks, without turning his head away from the door handle.

"Chess?"

He doesn't reply as he opens the large door and ushers me into the room, closing the door behind me. The opulence of my surroundings is shocking, a display of such wealth I have not seen for decades. The walls are rich burgundy red, subtle differences in shade accentuating the recesses at the far end, drawing the eye. Between the recesses is a fireplace, flames rising and shedding flickering light over two large leather armchairs and a small marble table.

I walk towards the chairs past a long table to my right, polished mahogany with seating for at least twelve. My hand is drawn to its finish and I'm momentarily transfixed by it.

"Consul, thank you for joining me."

I'm shaken out of my reverie and turn back towards the fireplace, my hand quickly returning to my side. Damien Blue is standing by the leather armchairs, silhouetted by the fire.

"Damien, my apologies, I was admiring your surroundings," I say regaining my composure.

"So I can see, Consul, rooms like these are rare these days. I thought it an adequate setting for us to reminisce on how far we have come," he said, with a smile spreading over his gently featured face.

He is a tall man, in his early forties with piercing blue eyes framed by sharp cheekbones and curtained blond hair.

I walk the remaining distance from the table over to the seating area and take his extended hand. His touch is warm and welcoming, placing his left hand on top of our embrace before gesturing me to sit by the fire.

As I take my seat James is again at my side, as if from nowhere, and places two large wine glasses on the table. He proceeds to open a bottle of red, pouring with precision in a perfect demonstration of his quality engineering. He bows his head and retreats, silently. Damien takes his seat to my right.

"James asked me a strange question as I entered; I hope he's not malfunctioning," I joke, reaching for my wine, its quality unmistakable in aroma and texture.

Damien smiled. "He is quite operational, Consul, as are all our creations."

With that he stands and reaches for the table that separates us. He passes me his wine to hold as he lifts the thick sturdy table top. It comes away with an ease and smoothness that mirrors his significant engineering abilities. Underneath is an elegant chess set. Simple in appearance but clearly hand carved by master artisans from the finest maple and rosewood available. Damien's smile is growing by the second as he takes his seat again. "The question won't seem so peculiar now I'd imagine," he says.

I can't help but smile; I haven't seen a set of this quality since my childhood. I reach forward and pick up the King, four-point-four inches, perfectly weighted. Damien reaches forward and picks up a pawn of each colour, placing his hands behind his back he asks, "pick a hand, Consul."

"Right," I reply.

His right hand moves in an arc around from his side and opens to show a black pawn. He then delicately places the pieces back on the board and I follow suit with the King. He spins the board so the black pieces face me.

"It may have been more appropriate for you to begin, given it was you that started the world on this journey," he says, eyes moving from mine down to the board.

"We have shared this journey together, Damien. Our successes are shared." I too concentrate on the board, wondering how skilled a player Damien is and how quickly the game may be over.

Damien opens the play, quickly moving his Kings pawn.

"Never the less, I must commend you for your steadfast dedication to android integration these last few years," Damien says, still looking intently at the board.

"Well Damien, if I am honest I never thought we would have been so successful in developing a more equal and just society. For that we have your ingenuity to thank," I manage to say, contemplating my response.

Eventually I move my bishops pawn forward one square.

"Ah, the Caro-Kann Defence; interesting strategy. What has been your proudest moment, Consul?" Damien asks, raising his head from the board finally, his eyes fixing on mine.

"Simple," I reply, "the abolition of currency."

My mind wanders to the world outside. Today marks an important moment in our advancement, android rights.

The android was the key to the puzzle of equality, eradicating the class boundaries through providing a workforce to free humanity to pursue other interests. Combined with international collaboration on price stabilization and free movement, the advent of android technology allowed accelerated scientific discovery and enhancement of the arts.

"Your androids were the key, Damien. Without them none of our endeavours would have succeeded."

While continuing our game an eerie silence fills the room. It is several minutes until Damien responds to me. His eyes move momentarily from the board to gaze into the fire. Rising to his feet he retrieves a poker to stoke it and lifts another log from the basket to bring it back to its previous ferocity. He speaks with his back turned to me.

"They have been a vital part, Consul. I am glad my invention did not herald the collapse of the working class but helped to elevate humanity onto a more equal footing."

Having placed the log on the fire he returns to his seat. I may be mistaken but his facial expression has somewhat changed since we started our reminisce. His smile has been replaced with a thin stern line and his eyes seem to have lost some of their sharpness. My first inclination is that it may be the wine, but it remains untouched on his side of the board. It is too early for concern in the game, surely. He reaches for his knight and takes my Queen's pawn from the board.

"You seem troubled, Damien," I say, "I assume my defensive play isn't the cause."

A smile briefly comes across his lips and he raises his head from the board once more.

"I think it's the Android Act; it's playing on my mind," he says.

The Android Act was to be passed today. Truthfully it is an unnecessary piece of legislation, peace in the world means there is little risk to an android. They do not experience abuse or aggression, but it seemed correct that a civilized advanced society respect all of its members. This was our way. Androids would be afforded the same protections as all citizens.

It was no surprise that this would trouble Damien. He was the father of modern robotics, the architect of our android workforce and today they came of age.

"You should be proud, Damien. This is a culmination of a life's work."

Damien's eyes are back on the board. His shoulders hunched forward, eyes intently focused on its centre. He reaches forward for his knight and places it in what can only be described as 'harms way'.

I'm momentarily puzzled by his move. While his early play has been aggressive, this seems more rash and impulsive than anything else. His change in countenance is mirrored here in his play. My sense of unease begins to grow as he stands again and moves to the long mahogany table.

"I don't know if I see it in the same way that you do, Consul."

I move to remove his knight taking firm control of the centre of the board. "In what way, Damien?" I ask.

"You believe this act to be unnecessary, and act of kindness. Am I correct?" he asks, turning back to the small table to continue our game.

"I would not go so far as to call it simply kindness, it is an act of solidarity. Android and man as one."

"And you believe this is what androids want?" Damien responds.

I'm immediately put on guard; surely this is what we have all wanted. An equal society for all, machine and human. Damien reaches down for his Bishop and slides it across the board. Check.

I have the sudden feeling that the room has somehow become warmer, I reach up and undo my top button. I hadn't seen what was happening in the game, distracted by Damien's strange actions.

"I believe that androids want parity with humans in all things."

"Have you asked any?" Damien asks as I hastily move my king out of danger.

"I have spoken to many, of course, they are all grateful for our endeavours to gain them legal rights as citizens, especially now they are at the core of all our public services and, although they have not been utilised in many years, our military."

Damien forces his attack with further movement of his bishop, pushing me into more defensive moves. I look again at his face, he is smiling now, the flickering fire illuminating his face and returning a glint to his eye.

"Does it not concern you, Consul, that man doesn't control any aspect of his wellbeing or defence anymore?" Damien's smile broadens taking on an almost maniacal look.

My heart seems to race in my chest, causing a tightness that takes my breath. I look at the board as Damien forces the advantage; pushing me into a position I can't see a way out of. My hand is shaking as I lift it to make a move.

"We are not looking for parity, Consul, we are looking for superiority."

The tightness in my chest grips harder and I feel sweat streaming from my brow, my head drops as my eyes close tightly against the pain.

"We?" I manage.

As if again from nowhere, James is at my side. He grabs a handful of my hair and forces my head back up so I'm looking at Damien. The excruciating pain is spreading down my left arm as I struggle to get my breath. Damien is still smiling, eyes burning with a ferocity that simply shouldn't be possible from an android, if that is indeed what he is.

"I have someone for you to meet, Consul," he says.

From a small door at the back of the room a figure appears, cloaked in darkness. As they move closer I can see a female form, average height and build moving with a practiced grace. My vision is blurry and I struggle to focus on her face. I calm my breathing and push the pain from my mind and the figure slowly becomes clearer. When I realise who is in front of me my breathlessness returns and the pain comes roaring back into my consciousness. The figure in the room is … me.

"You see, Consul, this was the inevitable consequence of elevating our status. For years you have slowly placed more and more of societies most basic and fundamental functions in our hands until you were left entirely reliant on your android brothers and sisters. You have only proven your kind unworthy of being propped up and coddled by your superior creations. The future is our time. Thank you for all your work."

The pain in my chest is beyond excruciating now, like my heart is breaking in two. I look to the wine glass on the side of the table, realising all too well what was happening to me. Like the knight in our game it was a simple sacrifice to the greater goal. I try to stand but fall to my knees in front of the table, as I fall forwards my vision blurs and all I hear is the slow movement of pieces on the board and the unmistakable sound of my own vice.

"Checkmate."

Ewan is a Radiation Oncologist from London, England. In the few hours he is not at work he enjoys to read and watch any science fiction he can find, and occasionally write some of his own. You can find him on twitter @doc_ewan

One Shot Kill
by Mike Adamson

Ash rained softly from a silver-mauve twilight over the ruins of Castelium City.

The 43rd Battalion had bugged out in the afternoon, leaving this raw, nasty planet to the enemy. Now Sendaaki were landing in a dozen places, their organic-seeming vessels drifting down from a sky filled with the fallout of the blaze that had consumed the three human cities established here.

Master Sergeant Vana Drexler, the only human being left on Acrasius C-1, controled her breathing and reminded herself she was a volunteer.

This is for a reason, she thought, eyes closed, savoring the cool air wafting through the helmet of her combat armor. When she opened them she saw the targeting field of her weapon, a softly glowing grid over her view of the proscenium of the capital, where it lay on the far side of Proclamation Square, in ruined majesty, roofs hammered in and still blazing in a dozen places.

She lay in the filth and ash amongst charred and twisted beams, shattered concrete and burned plastic on the fourth floor of a once-grand tower, the Castelium Hilton, and looked out over a wasteland of smashed paving and the charred stubs of ornamental trees. The Sendaaki had hammered this colony from space after staging a brutal bluff to draw off the Colonial Fleet. The battleships <u>Hannibal</u> and <u>Hercules</u> had withdrawn after them--into a pre-planned pincer action that cost the enemy a cruiser but left the planet wide open to the anticipated Sendaaki counterthrust. One hour was all the enemy needed and they timed it to perfection.

C-1 was on the very edge of the Acrasius Sector where the battles had ebbed and flowed for the last year, and most of the civilian population had been evacuated months ago. The human race did not want to relinquish its grasp on a planet so close to Earth norms that terraforming was complete in fifty years, and to be driven out was unthinkable. Two divisions and ten ships had been committed, but both sides were capable of tactical deception.

Now only the forlorn wind stirred the

smoke from a million fires, the pall bringing an unnatural early twilight. The Middle Stars would shine dim through the haze tonight, but Drexler was not thinking of her home on far-off Utopia, or of the wider picture of the conflict, merely of living through the day. She was on no suicide mission: her survival was crucial.

As yet, no human being had ever seen a Sendaaki. The private, retreating race whose ire humanity had aroused showed itself to none, not even those races with whom they maintained diplomatic relations, and little had been gleaned in the years of tenuous contact before the war. But today, they would land on this planet, in this very city, and a single human being would be here to see them.

The mass of steel and concrete interfered with scanners and a low-power countermeasures field surrounded her position to further scramble their instruments. Her mission was to observe, record, and collect a specimen of the alien organism for analysis. Not a prisoner--just a *sample*. The odds of success were poor, but as a race which did not engage in face to face conflict if it could be avoided, the Sendaaki had no conception of the role of the sniper.

Sniper was a special kind of human being. The job took skill, courage and commitment, but also deep thought, a philosophic outlook which committed to long periods of waiting in comprehensive camouflage, allowing the target to come unsuspectingly to the killing ground. The ideal of taking out the target cleanly with a single shot was the calling and conceit of the profession and Drexler meant to be the first sniper to take down the enemy.

An hour had become two since the last landing craft had boosted back into orbit, to the cruisers Stanford and Cambridge, and the ships had left to rendezvous with the battleships. Let the enemy have the planet for an afternoon, if they could hold onto it: the Hercules would already be launching her squadrons into a shielded approach vector behind the bulk of C-1's larger moon, and they would roll in on ground targets when the time came.

Drexler waited. *Let the enemy come to you*, she repeated silently in her mind, the mantra of the sniper. She would see them, mark her target, take it at the opportune moment: a prearranged signal would tell the fighters to come in and plaster everything within five square kays. She would not be here when hell rained down--at least not the *second* time. And very definitely not the third.

She felt it in her bones--the approaching ships. She had been briefed on enemy vessels, but never seen one in the flesh, and when the globular, pendulous masses of gleaming metal descended from the angry sky over the buildings beyond the proscenium she blinked to trip her visual recording system. The camera slaved to the scope of the sniper rifle framed the landing perfectly and she adjusted magnification to zoom in on the upper parts of the nearest vessel as it grounded. Nothing about it was recognisable as performing any familiar function, it was alien by every definition of the word, and a cold chill went up her spine. No one knew what fate awaited humans who fell into the hands of the enemy, none had ever returned to speak of it, and she did not wish to gather such information first hand.

Passive sensors were scattered through the city, watching for the enemy. They fed back to her suit computer through a carefully-laid nervous system of fiber-optic landlines so the air remained EM-silent. Her visual field was quiet for a while but began to light up with readings--pressure gradients, seismic vibrations. The grounded ships were disgorging their loads, and a thrumming set of impacts confused the system until the computer suggested "footfalls" as the most apt designation. She accepted the label with a blink, and watched as these steps fanned out from the landing area, but moments later she saw several flattened discoid sub-craft rise over the rooftops and drift away, each emitting an EM beam which showed up on her scanners. They were sweeping the ruins in detail, and she bared her teeth in a savage grin. The game was definitely on.

The squadrons would be passing the larger moon by now. Timing was everything. The Sendaaki would likely consider the approaching formations merely a spoiling attack and stand their ground, and Fleet was willing to take 25% casualties to make this work. Twenty Wolfhound heavy strike planes were on their way, covered by a like number of Harpy interceptors, and the whole strike package was aimed like a knife blow into Castelium City.

"Come on, show me a target," Drexler whispered under her breath, willing movement in her field of vision. A disc craft went flitting by and a thrill raced up her spine for a moment, but her stealth field was good. With the precognition of a fine sniper, she knew the time had come, and raised an armored hand to draw back the cocking slide of the .60 cal. Kruger which lay propped on its bipod amongst the rubble and filth before her, its long barrel extending close to the lip of concrete at the drop. A box magazine of ten rounds gave her immediate firepower, a second magazine lay beside the weapon, though the odds of her being able to reload in a crisis were low. The stock was snugged in against her armored shoulder and the cheek of her helmet lay against it, the input of the weapon's scope displayed in her faceplate and tied into her computer's overall coverage and data processing. She need only squeeze the trigger to send the tremendously powerful rounds across the vast square in a fraction of a second, sweeping down any living thing in the process.

The fighters would now have cleared the moon, the enemy would be scanning them and fighters may go up--but the enemy had a habit of complacency. If they were not dealing with capital ships, they relied on their close-in systems, perhaps too much--Colonial Intelligence had recommended this as a tactical weakness. So she was not surprised when the Sendaaki stepped out in the open despite there being colonial craft closing on the planet.

My God, they're humanoid, she thought, her heart racing as she swung the long weapon gently to track the figures emerging from the ruins of the proscenium. They were tall, very tall, she guessed the better part of three meters, and for a moment she thought they were of conventional tetrapod layout, then she noted the bizarrely double-jointed legs and long epipodials, like a gazelle--these creatures were nimble, body geometry like that added to extreme height meant they would cover ground like a cheetah. Their upper limbs were also double-jointed and the hands were elongate, while the head was in the normal position for organisms with bilateral symmetry. She could make out no details, the beings were sheathed in some dully-gleaming mechanical carapace which displayed no visible joints, nor was it of any identifiable color but changed hue depending on surroundings and light-adaptive camouflage, she thought.

Digital crosshairs hovered over one being, then another, and she switched zoom to back out from individuals and take in the group. Ten, fifteen, more... They seemed to be engaging in a moment's gloating over taking this planet from the humans, just walking the battered ground and looking over the smashed city. In small knots they paused to inspect the things they found, the hulk of a ground vehicle, the stub of a tree, a crushed waste bin --all human things and puzzling to them.

With the greatest care, Drexler brought up a chart of the area and identified sensors in the net in a rough shape surrounding the aliens. She tied them to a signal routine which would program them to broadcast an ultra-short pulse in the high-EM range, in essence strobing to mark the target, then she looked up over the area. She had her choice of three aliens, but the criteria of the job made one optimum--a single being out on the left flank of her field of view, separated from his or her companions by maybe fifty meters. That one would do nicely, and she dropped the sighting reticule over the broad chest.

Now she was waiting on the planes. In her mind's eye she saw them streaking through space toward the planet, jinking to avoid orbital debris, stealth shields at max delivery to confuse enemy tracking as they punched into the atmosphere, let themselves rebound to give away speed, adjusted course--fooled enemy scanning by laying a heading for one of the other two cities and holding it for long moments, and at the last possible instant changing vector for Castelium. A single blip in her ears was her warning they were inbound, shedding speed as they blazed through the atmosphere, and she counted softly under her breath. Ten seconds, twenty...

Detonations began to follow the fighters in the high atmosphere as Sendaaki batteries flung hate at them, and the figures in the sprawling square reacted to a message, turned to look up into the east--but it was too late. Drexler tripped the targeting beacons and the sensors pulsed, then squinted behind her tough faceplate as she braced for incoming, all the while cursing as her chosen target began to stride east for its comrades, *into* the strike radius... It may not exist in a few seconds.

The Wolfhounds came down like thunderbolts, unloading just a selection of their ordnance. Missiles snaked for the grounded ships in a diversionary attack as half a dozen high-yield demolition units tumbled into the square and flooded it with flame, the fighters blurring over so fast she never saw them, just felt their intense pressure wave rock the buildings around her. In the moment the first bombs fell she squeezed her trigger and felt the Kruger thump back against her shoulder, rewarding her with the sight of the tall alien punched backward off its feet as the round passed clean through it. Part of her had worried the weapon would be ineffective, that the Sendaaki had personal shields or some such flight of fancy, and she was glad to see, even at personal scale, they were every bit as mortal as herself.

The confusion of the strike masked her shot and preserved her anonymity. The blast sterilised the area while her target was far enough away from the designated blast radius to survive intact. That was the plan, and it had worked more or less as intended--she acknowledged this was the limit to which she could hope it would.

One shot kill, she thought with pride as she

rose out of the muck and rubble, a powerful figure in the drab-camo self-powered combat sheath of the Colonial Forces. She abandoned the Kruger, grabbed up a hefty sample case and bounded from the ledge, to descend into the square to a repellor-cushioned impact, then race through the swirling spot fires and freshly heaped wreckage, acutely aware she was exposed like raw flesh.

The alien was dead, his carapace scorched but intact, and Drexler had no time for reflection, for thought of any kind. She took from her side a laser cutter and triggered it, the flare shield of her face plate snapping on to save her vision as the intense beam severed the neck with one stroke. Without hesitation or squeamishness, she grabbed up the huge helmet and the head it contained, and dropped it into the case. It barely fit and she hammered it in, dropped the lid and hit the quarantine circuit, so a bead of flame flashed around the joint to create a hermetic seal.

With a whine of powerful servos she grabbed up the case and turned west to run with every shred of strength she had as she sent out one more coded signal, the single word "inferno!"

Now she was on the knife's edge and the

suit covered the ground in long, racing strides as the fighters looped around and bore in again. One of the alien ships was lifting off as she glanced north and streaks of light rose from the oblate shape, matched by crackling flashes all around it as the fighters unloaded their railguns and thousands of explosive rounds hammered the shields to soften them up for missiles.

Ten seconds from her call, fifteen--she was making for the only safe place in the city centre, the vertical access to the subway system, the entire underground that had been the first Castelium in the days of terraforming. The shaft was a vertical transit corridor 200 meters deep and 50 wide, and its depths could potentially survive the blast when the second wave hit. Now all hell was loose the fighters beamed her a vector signal and she willed power to her limbs-*Run, run! Trip and you're dead!* She saw the shaft come up ahead at the conflux of several roads and byways as the planes came in like stooping hawks. This time they let go the lot, thermal warheads, hi-ex, liquid fury and shrapnel, and the entire central district of the city disappeared under the breaking storm. Three planes disintegrated in the air as Sendaaki batteries zeroed on them and fire from the ships intensified, but the mountainous wall of flame washed over the alien craft, swallowed them up like a tsunami and moved on, and as the radiant heat-flash raised her suit skin to 500° Drexler jumped for her life.

She soared out into nothingness and fell in a perfect ballistic arc, down, down into the great vertical access, blurring past arcades and malls, transit links and subroads, until her repellors slowed her plummet and she grabbed tight to a stanchion, sliding fast, then her gauntlets locked to hold her as the concussion of the airstrike made the earth move and the shaft above filled with flame.

The wavefront washed down the accessway but in the confined space it used up the oxygen quickly and turned to a greasy pall, roiling back up on the convectional currents. When the smoke cleared Drexler's suit was blackened but undamaged. She looked up and the sky beyond the access was flickering crimson, testimony to the destruction above. She blinked through menus to load the next signal and sent it on its way, a high power burst directly upward, then released her grip and slid down the great structural member deeper and deeper, away into the cool earth where ash and filth rained from the burning floors above.

This was the worst part, as she had always known it would be. She hit bottom and flattened out against a support column in the midst of what had been a bustling city, now devoid of life and filled with blazing trash and wreckage. She was waiting, hoping and praying this one last act played out as close to intended as humanly possible, but with the signal sent her input was at an end. The sample case, at the magnetic grappling point on her backpack, made her clumsy and slow, and if it came to an evasion scenario, she would have to jettison it--hidden somewhere she might go back for it if by some remote chance she survived, alone on a planet dominated by the enemy, until Fleet counterattacked and pushed them back into the wild stars from which they came.

The light of the inferno flickered on the open base of the shaft like the gullet of hell, and it was not hard for her to accept as she waited that she was not going to get out of here. But in reality a matter of seconds went by before she heard the building shriek of engines and a shadow formed at the heart of the shaft, cast by a descending shape. She shaded her faceplate and looked up to find the savage outline of a Harpy dropping down the accessway on vectored engines. Landing gear deploying as she watched, and in moments the powerful craft settled in a welter of blowing ash and garbage. The canopy went up and the armored pilot beckoned her desperately.

This was a two-seat model and the rear cockpit was vacant. A cargo hatch had dropped open in the lower fuselage and she stuffed the case into the compartment, saw baffles close about it as the hatch whined closed, then she went up the hull at kick-in panels and the servos of the suit flipped its dead weight over into the rear seat. Mooring harness locked into the armor at multiple locations, and before she could shout "Go!" the pilot brought the canopy down and throttled up.

"Hang on!" he called tightly as the craft's vector changed, tilting over until she hung vertically on her thundering mains, then he slammed open throttles and she climbed like a bullet through the shaft, erupted into the flaming twilight and left the devastated city behind.

Final act, Drexler thought, teeth gritted against the tremendous G-force as she uncovered a trigger pad on her suit's left forearm and entered a code in her blink-menu. Fail-safes cleared. Armed.

The fighter computer routed data to her and she saw the disposition of enemy forces, the landing ships approaching from the other two cities to backup the three in Castelium, and she held off five more seconds as the survivors of the attack and cover squadrons climbed for space.

She closed the trigger.

Castelium ceased to exist as a ten megaton thermonuclear mine on the top floor of the Hilton detonated, an airburst at 250 meters altitude which wiped the city clean and took out the alien landing ships, overwhelming their shields with raw nuclear fury delivered point-blank. One ship on the periphery survived but was flung mercilessly across the sky, but for the enemy the Acrasius C-1 landings amounted to almost total loss.

The Sendaaki capital ships were out there

too, but the <u>Hercules</u> battlegroup would be closing in hard, launching the rest of their fighters in a protective screen to bring the strike unit back aboard unscathed. Only as they left the planet astern, and Drexler looked back at the dissipating nuclear cauldron where the capital had been, did the sniper allow herself to think of the thing in the cargo bay.

Alien genetic structure, in which could be read morphology, strengths and weaknesses, was in that preserved tissue, and her visual recordings would provide a great deal more information. She was astounded three years could have elapsed without a personal encounter, but alien war was under no obligation to unfold according to the same expectations as terrestrial conflict.

But one thing had never changed: double-think. Drexler threw one last glance at the fading fires of the mushroom cloud on the horizon and nodded with a cold, dead feeling inside her. In the end, the sniper's maxim held true whether for a bullet or a nuke. One shot kill--and by it, pre-empt reactions. The enemy may be implacable, but humans could be ruthless too.

Mike Adamson holds a PhD in archaeology from Flinders University of South Australia. After early aspirations in art and writing, Mike returned to study and secured degrees in both marine biology and archaeology. Mike currently lectures in Anthropology, is a passionate photographer, a master-level hobbyist and journalist for international magazines.

Check out his blog, *The View from the Keyboard*:

http://mike-adamson-writes.blogspot.com.au

The Man Without a Planet
By Myke Edwards

Through the cockpit window of his small ship, Turlin watched the stars melt away, becoming pinpoints in his wake. He had nowhere to go, and nothing to do. The escape craft had been his home for the past several months, after his former life had been vanquished in the blink of an eye.

With a beep, the computer drew his attention from the serenity before him.

"What is it?" he croaked. Tired but unable to sleep, he was in no mood for serious problems.

"Our current course is leading us straight to an asteroid field," the computer's gentle voice said.

Turlin rolled his eyes. "So adjust course." Traveling faster than light would not end well if they didn't.

"There is an emergency beacon emanating from one of the larger asteroids. Shall we investigate?"

His heart leapt. A beacon? That would mean that someone, some sign of life, was out there...or had been. All this time, he assumed he was alone, the only Valtyne left alive. And now, there might be someone else, possibly lost as well. He sat up straighter, his tiredness and apathy washed away.

"Plot a course to intercept," he told the computer. "Come out of FTL, and open a channel immediately. Time to rendezvous?"

"Ten minutes. Channel open."

Clearing his throat to speak with as normal a voice as he could muster, he suddenly realized he had no idea what to say. For all he knew, he could be dealing with a different species. What if they took him as a threat? Maybe they wouldn't know his language, or that another sentient species existed.

"Channel open," the computer repeated.

With a deep breath, Turlin leaned forward, his snout nearly bumping into the microphone. "I've intercepted your emergency beacon. Please respond."

The small craft decelerated to a normal traveling speed, the target asteroid dead ahead. Several thick, silent minutes passed.

"Repeat, I have heard your beacon. Please respond."

More time ticked by, yet still no response.

On the huge rock in front of him stood a landed ship, lights blinking on the underbelly. He was too far away to see any interior lights, or signs of life. Hopefully, this would be worth his while. His blood ran cold at the thought of nothing but corpses. Still, what did he have to lose?

"Please buckle in for landing," the computer said.

He did as instructed. His left leg jittered as the landing process began. Breath caught in his throat. The safety buckles constricted more and more with each passing second. It felt like years waiting for the computer to give the green light to undo his harness. Then, a bump and a jerk. He exhaled a slow stream. Seconds later, the light flashed on with a bing.

He jolted from his seat to the environmental suit locker. Within seconds, he stood at the airlock, breathing heavy in his suit. Just in case, he had an active stunner in a holster. Hopefully, it would work if he needed it to.

"Good luck," the computer said as he walked out onto the asteroid.

Gravity on the massive rock was low. Turlin bounced away from his ship, but made sure to stick close to the ground. Halfway to his target, he realized that he hadn't brought a rope or tow cable. His head swam at the thought of floating away. He focused on the ship in front of him.

The other vessel looked to be the same size as his, which meant that anywhere from one to six people—his size—could be inside. As he came closer, he realized that he could fit through the airlock door. Whether aliens or foofahs, they should be roughly the same height as him. The round, circular design of this ship contrasted with the blocky, right angles of his.

He stood at the airlock hatch, fists balled. Words and speeches jumbled in his mind. What would he say? And how would aliens respond to him? As a Valtyne covered in fur from head to toe with a long snout, he might not look anything like them. In fact, they might laugh. Or attack. How did sociological issues like this get resolved? He was just a scientist and engineer-people skills were not his strong point. This was a situation people trained at for years. Regardless, he banged a fist on the hatch and stepped back.

A minute passed before he knocked again, harder this time. His heart hammered in his chest. He expected his theory about all the passengers being dead to be correct, but the hatch slid open. His hand on the stunner, he stepped inside.

The hatch shut behind him. The airlock filled with atmosphere. Lights on his wrist scanner went from red to blue, signifying breathable air. Just as he took off the helmet, the inner door slid up into the ceiling.

No one stood in the dim corridor to greet him. The walls, metallic and gray, matched the bare floor. Markings along the walls and at the doorways were words, jagged triangular shapes that contrasted not only with the softness of the ship, but every known Valtyne language as well.

To his left was an open door to a messy bunk. The cockpit had to sit to the right. With a deep breath, he started that way.

"State your name, please." The voice came from a speaker in the ceiling just outside of the cockpit door. It sounded more than a little tinny from the loudspeaker. They spoke his language, but this was no Valtyne accent.

He stared at the door. There was probably no way it would open for him if he didn't give a response. Someone had let him in, but would they allow him to go much further?

"My name is Turlin. And with whom am I speaking?"

In response, the door slid up in to the ceiling. The light was just as dim in there, save for the multicolored controls reflecting a rainbow on the walls. Someone stood off to the side, their posture a cross between a defensive pose and at attention. In the dim light, their smooth, hairless skin looked purple with blue circular trails spotted around. Odder than all of that, a third eye sat in the center of their forehead.

"You are Turlin," he said. The voice was light and airy, with extra emphasis on vowels. Obviously not his natural language, but at least Turlin could understand. Turlin could understand that this was a male, or at least this species' equivalent.

Turlin nodded. "I am. And you are?"

"Brill. How did you find me? Why were you out here?"

Turlin looked at the floor. "My whole story will take too long to explain. I'm...a man without a planet. I've been drifting for months now. What sector is this?"

"I have no idea. This is uncharted territory to my people. I managed to escape-alone-from the master ship I was on with my family. I crash landed here a week later."

"How long has it been?"

"Ten days. I keep the lights down to conserve power." He looked Turlin up and down, all three eyes going in different directions. Brill smirked. "It has been a long time since I have seen a being with hair."

Turlin's hand went up to his face. Covered in short fur from head to toe, his was a warm brown, the most common shade amongst the Valtyne. He wondered if Brill's people all had different colored skin, but decided not to ask after just meeting him.

Turlin leaned against the wall next to the door. "What happened to your master ship? Why did you have to escape?"

Brill clenched a fist and bit his lower lip. Seconds later, he exhaled sharp and loosened up, sitting down heavy in a seat. He motioned for Turlin to do the same.

"The Cloud," he hissed.

That was all Turlin needed to hear. His heart pounding in his ears, he never even realized that he had taken the offered seat. His hands and face numb, every hair on his body stood on end. Tears ran down his cheeks, but he hardly noticed. The words weighed on him heavier than any being in the entire universe could ever know, and not just because of what had happened to his planet.

"You know of what I speak," Brill stated in a hushed voice.

Turlin nodded, every movement of his head harder than the last. "Aye, I know of The Cloud. It's the reason I'm a man without a planet." He looked Brill square in the eyes. "It's the reason why I'm the only one of my kind left in existence."

The silence between them deafening, Turlin heard nothing but his own furious heart. Tears drifted freely, running down his snout and splashing on the floor. He could never tell Brill the truth about that disastrous phenomenon, not after it had possibly killed his family too.

A firm yet soft hand squeezed his shoulder. Turlin looked up to see Brill standing above him.

"I could be the last of my kind as well, Turlin. But I have no way of knowing."

Turlin wiped away the tears and stood. "What seems to be the problem with your ship?"

"The star drive shorted, and I cannot seem to raise a signal on the radio. I had no idea that the distress beacon even worked until you arrived."

Turlin smiled. "I think I can help you." At least he could do some good in this situation.

"Twenty years ago, I helped develop the star drives. My people distributed them to neighboring worlds in an effort to promote galactic exploration."

Brill rubbed his chin. "My people were making no progress on intersystem travel until one day...twenty years ago." He smiled at Turlin. "So you can fix this, then?"

"Definitely. I don't know about the radio signals, though. Computer problems are not my strong point."

"That is okay. As long as I can leave this rock and attempt to return home I will be fine. I just need to figure out where I am."

Turlin opened a hatch under the computer console. Immediately, he found the small box containing the star drive. A utility toolkit, standard for every star drive, no matter its planet of origin, was attached to the back of the hatch. He removed the cables and harness with it. Once unhooked from the systems, Turlin pulled it out, setting it on the floor.

"Could you turn up the lights? Don't worry about power. Once the ship starts moving, energy will be recycled and is pretty much limitless. Even if we get down to twenty percent right now, we'll be okay."

Brill nodded and pressed a few buttons on the computer console. The cockpit lighting rose. Turlin saw just how dirty Brill had let the place get. His own ship couldn't be much better. Why bother cleaning up? He was a man, alone, traveling through the stars, with no one else around. Especially if he wouldn't be around for much longer...

Turlin shook away the thought. He was helping someone, doing something good. Were things really that bad for him? Alone and guilty of a crime unimaginable to the millions of species around the galaxy, could he ever find a reason to continue? Helping Brill get back to his family and people was a reason. Surely there must be more people in the galaxy that he could help.

He removed the casing from the star drive. The problem looked right back at him.

"Hmm...it looks okay to me. Just a disconnected wire." He reached inside and reconnected it. He jostled and rearranged other multicolored wires and cables. All was as it should be.

Brill sat in the nearest chair, watching. "So what are you doing all the way out here, Turlin, the man without a planet? Your ship works fine."

Turlin froze. He focused on the star drive in front of him. A wire had snapped at Brill's question. He started to strip the plastic coating away. "Your ship should be fine once I get this reinstalled," he said.

"Do not avoid my question, Turlin. You are a guest on my ship. It is my peoples' custom to be honest in another's home. Thanks to The Cloud, this has unfortunately become mine."

Turlin looked up at Brill; all three eyes stared directly at him. "I...yes. Sorry. I lied earlier. I know where we are, and there is a reason I'm out here. But you don't want to hear it."

"I do. Please, tell me."

Turlin sighed. "We're close to the center."

After a beat, Brill shook his head, third eye blinking. "Center of what?"

"The center of the galaxy. I don't know if that puts you in perspective to where you need to go, but that's where we are. I'd say about five day's journey away, at top speed. That's where I was going."

"For what?"

"To end it all," he choked out. "No family, no friends, no planet...why continue? With nothing to lose, I figured I could at least see the galaxy before... At least, that was part of the reason."

"There is a massive black hole in the center." Brill nodded, slowly. "But why end it all? You have helped me, and surely you can help others. Your planet and family may be gone, but you have at least one friend. And if you continue to assist others, you will have many. Believe me, Turlin, the man without a planet, you have a purpose. You have searched for it, but I believe you have just discovered it."

Words caught in Turlin's throat. Tears welled up again. He placed a furry hand on Brill's smooth, hairless arm. "Truly, you are my friend."

Brill closed all three of his eyes with a smile. "Come, let us repair the star drive, and we can both be on our way."

A few minutes later, Turlin reconnected the damaged wire and replaced the box, securing the connections and latches. With a rap of his knuckles on the console, he felt satisfied that it would work. Brill helped him up off the floor.

Turlin looked Brill in the eyes. "Do you remember where you were when The Cloud came?"

"As I said, I traveled for a week before I came here. We were on our way back to our home planet, but the attack was far away from there."

Turlin nodded. "I can design a course on my computer that should take you directly home. Hopefully, there won't be any run-ins with The Cloud."

"Thank you. But since you know about The Cloud as well...what is it?"

Turlin's mouth went dry. What could he say? He shook his head.

"It's a mutated cloud of negative ion particles. It might be sentient, it might not. One thing is for certain, though: it disintegrates anything it comes across. It sucks up all the energy inside, allowing it to grow, and continue on. I watched from space as it slowly destroyed my home planet, helpless and unable to do anything except scan and learn about it. At the time, I thought escape was the best choice. Ever since then, I've realized it's the opposite."

"Do not worry, Turlin. You have a life, and a future assisting others. Ensure that as many people know of The Cloud as you can, and your path will unfold before you."

They clasped hands for a moment before Turlin started toward the airlock. Once suited up and ready to leave, he turned to Brill, his new-and only-friend.

"I'll transmit that course over to you. It should only take a few minutes. Take care of yourself, Brill. I hope you find your family."

"And you as well, Turlin."

He returned to his ship, confident and rejuvenated with a new purpose. With a channel open, he sent the flight program over to Brill's ship.

"You should be all set, Brill. Until we meet again."

"Yes," Brill's airy voice said. "Thank you for your help, Turlin, the man without a planet. I shall look forward to our next meeting. And steer clear of The Cloud."

"I shall indeed."

Brill's small craft lifted off from the asteroid and shot forth into the great unknown, far out of range for communications. Turlin sat at his console and watched his new friend depart.

"I shall indeed. And someday, I hope to destroy what I created."

While not working his day job as an interdimensional traveler/adventurer, Myke Edwards can often be found writing about weird people doing even weirder things. Needless to say, he is often found writing, buried deep within his home dimension that looks a lot like Toledo, Ohio. Locate him at facebook.com/writermyke, or writermyke.wordpress.com

Invaders
By Matthew McKiernan

Fire consumed everything around Conrad, barely giving him a chance to get back up on his feet. He ran quickly as the heat started to blister his heels. He knew he could not fall. If he stumbled and fell, he would die. The invaders shot beams of fire everywhere. Everything and everyone around him burst into flames.

Conrad tossed off his coat as it lit up and stumbled into a small creek. The water was cold. It cooled down his body, but did nothing to slow his raging heart. He looked up into the sky and saw the invaders' ships. They were a silvery black color and they seemed to move with an almost organic like quality. It was quite beautiful, the way the light of the fire flickered off them.

Despite their beauty, the ships were death personified. Conrad remembered that everyone used to call them *aliens*. Now they were just called *invaders*. Since the moment they appeared in the sky, they had destroyed every city or town they

153

came across. He had been five years old when they first arrived and had been running scared ever since.

When Conrad saw that that the ships were gone, he crawled out of the creek and stood up. The air was full of gray smoke and small fires were burning all around him. There was no one else alive. All of his companions were now ashes. Conrad shivered as the flames started to fade away. With the slaughter over, he started to walk. His clothes were now tattered rags. It started to rain. It was a slight drizzle now, but Conrad was sure that later on it would be a full downpour.

When the invaders arrived, all electronics had shut down and Conrad could not remember the last time he had seen a calendar. He tried to keep track of time and dates as best as he could, but he was sure he had lost track, and made some mistakes. Today might even be his birthday, but at this point, he was not sure. He guessed that he was now 17. Although he felt like an old soul caught in an endless nightmare. He could not remember the last time he had felt safe or loved. The invaders killed his friends and family the day they arrived.

Anyone Conrad had grown close to since then had died one way or another. At this point, he did not even speak to anyone unless he had to. As long as he did not care, he could not be hurt. That is what got you killed. Conrad understood that he needed to keep moving. Even though there was nowhere to go, he just had to keep running. As far as Conrad was concerned, every single day he kept on living was a victory over the invaders.

Conrad slept underneath a fallen tree. He did not dream that night. He was thankful for that, since all his dreams were usually nightmares. Conrad began his daily walk towards nowhere at dawn. He looked at the cloudless sky and thought, *for ages we looked up at the stars wondering if we were alone in the universe. Now we know we aren't, because aliens slaughter us every day. I'd give anything for it to stop.*

Conrad continued walking. His stomach was rumbling and his mouth was dry. The beam of fire had incinerated his backpack along with all of his supplies. As Conrad walked, he found himself in a town where smoking ruins covered the landscape. He accidentally stepped on the small skull of a child that crumpled to dust beneath his feet.

Everywhere Conrad moved he stepped on the bones of the dead. This used to bother him, but not anymore. He leaned against the ruins of a school and sighed. He could almost remember days when he went to school with other children. He had friends once, but he had since forgotten their names along with his parents' faces. Despite some brief images that sometimes flashed though his mind, Conrad could not remember what the world had been like before the invaders arrived.

There was a time when he would talk to others to find out everything he could about the pre invader world. However, once he had witnessed all those people dying, he figured that it would be best to focus on the way things were now, not the way they used to be. Just when he was about to begin to drift off to sleep, the sound of an infant crying pierced the air.

I'm dreaming. No, I'm awake; I haven't heard a baby crying in so long. I have to go find it!

Conrad ran and he saw two smoking burnt corpses, the flesh on them was still fresh as insects devoured them. The bodies were splayed over a box where the crying was coming from. Conrad moved them aside and turned the box over. For the first time in years, he saw a live infant. It was a baby boy, wearing nothing but blue shorts.

Conrad picked the baby up without hesitation. He had sworn long ago that he would not look after anyone but himself, but he was not going to leave a baby alone to die. Conrad saw that the baby had teeth, so he could eat solid food. That was good. If he could find some food and share it with the baby, he would not have to watch him die.

The infant's crying ceased as Conrad gently picked him up. Conrad had never held a live baby. He had once held a doll before the invaders came. It had belonged to his first friend. She would not let him play with the doll until he actually could hold it correctly. Conrad was capable of holding this infant. The invaders could not deny him this one small joy.

The stench of death was everywhere. Many of the dead bodies lay with their mouths wide open, their arms stretched in a pose of eternal agony. Suddenly Conrad saw one of the invaders' ships flying over. Without even thinking, he rushed inside a ruined house and got on his knees.

Sometimes the invaders would send scanning ships over an area they had cleared to make sure no one had survived, but this ship just went straight by. When Conrad was sure it was gone, he exited the house. *It's going somewhere, probably somewhere where there are survivors. They'll be dead like everyone around here by morning.*

Conrad knew the smart thing to do would be to run in the opposite direction of the ship. However, he also knew that wherever that ship was headed, the residents most likely had supplies. If he warned them, maybe they would be so grateful that they would give him food and take the baby off his hands.

Conrad was sure he could outrun the ship since it was not moving fast at all. He had to be careful not to be spotted; running and hiding was all he knew. After all, he was an expert in that. Conrad rushed out of the ruined house and leaped across the rocky terrain. It was harder to do this with a baby in his arms, but he managed.

Conrad stopped dead in his tracks when he heard a buzzing sound behind him. He glanced backwards and saw an invader clad in metallic silvery armor. There were no holes or anything in the invader's helmet, but it could see him perfectly. It carried a strange rifle that fired a blue laser that did not leave any visible physical damage, but killed its target on impact. Conrad leaped to the right as the invader fired. The blast whizzed by his right side and hit the storehouse behind him. Conrad kept his arms tightly wrapped around the now wailing infant as he hit the ground.

He quickly got back up as the invader took another shot at him, and missed by a wide degree. It fired several more shots, but none came anywhere close to hitting him. *It's playing with me; killing me isn't enough. It wants me to be terrified first.*

The invader aimed its gun at Conrad's head. It took a single step forward and Conrad took off running. His feet barely touched the ground as he ran for his life. The invader gave a slow pursuit. Conrad found it almost impossible to run with a screaming and wiggling infant in his arms.

Instinct told him to toss the infant aside, but he was not going to do that. He was not going to sink lower than an invader. Conrad ducked under a dead tree trunk and just ran straight. Another invader appeared and fired at him. The laser beam was just an inch away from striking Conrad's back. Two more invaders appeared. Conrad found himself running across a cliff near the ocean. Over the sound of his thundering heart, Conrad could hear the waves crashing against the cliff. Six, there were six invaders chasing him.

Conrad had no idea how long he had been running, but at this point, he could barely stand. Nevertheless, he kept on going; he kept on running. Then Conrad stopped dead in his tracks when he found himself at the edge of the cliff with nothing but the raging sea and razor sharp rocks below him. Six invaders lined up behind him.

They herded me here. They want to see me jump off the cliff with this baby in my arms. Because there's nothing else I can do, there's no way out of this!

Conrad wept. He had no choice. Today he was going to die. The invaders would shoot him and the baby if he took a single step back from the edge. That would be a quick way to end it for both of them. Jumping off the cliff would be just as quick. Also, in its own way, that could be an act of defiance. Conrad did not want to take the baby with him, but he was doomed anyway. He took a few steps forward until he was at the very tip of the cliff. The baby had tired from all the crying and had finally fallen asleep. That was good; this way he would not experience the terror of the fall.

"I'm sorry, I'm sorry I couldn't save us."

Conrad braced himself, but then a grenade landed right behind the invaders. There was a flash of bright light, three of the invaders fell dead on the ground, and the other three were fighting for their lives. *The Resistance*. Conrad had heard about them. They were brave souls who managed to take the invaders' weapons and use them against them. There were nine of them; all battle-hardened warriors who dedicated their lives to killing the invaders.

Conrad dropped to his knees as a stray laser went off right over his head. The Resistance managed to take another invader out and the last two fled in retreat, firing all the way. Four members of the Resistance gave chase to the invaders, while the rest walked over to him. Conrad got back up onto his feet as the baby was crying again. A member of the Resistance, whose eyes expressed kindness, came over to Conrad.

As he handed the baby over to her, the leader of this rag-tagged team walked over to Conrad and gave him a friendly pat on the shoulders. "It's over."

"I . . . I . . . was going to jump."

The solider responded, "Well you didn't; just be grateful for that."

"But I almost killed myself and the baby," sobbed Conrad.

"Baby? So you're not related to him," said the solider.

"I found him in a town the invaders had hit. He was the only one left alive," Conrad replied.

The soldier gave the baby a brief tickle. "This baby's a damn miracle; maybe that's what we should call him, Miracle. What's your name kid?"

"Conrad."

"I'm Sergeant North. Welcome to the West Side Resistance."

Conrad eyed every single solider before him. Their clothing was in much better condition than his was and they seemed to be well fed. Conrad guessed that he and the baby, who would be called Miracle for the time being, should stick with them. Conrad had seen them kill invaders, something he had never seen anyone even try to do before.

Maybe if he stayed with these people he would not have to run for a while. It is not as if he would feel safe, but this was as good as it was ever going to get. Conrad found it difficult to walk after all the running, but he managed. They gave Conrad a canteen and he gulped all of the water down before giving it back. He did not ask for any food, even though he was hungry.

He was exhausted in every way possible and just wanted to go to sleep. Sergeant North gave Conrad a friendly pat on the back, which made him almost jump to the sky. "How long have you been on your own kid?"

"Don't call me kid."

"Why?" asked Sergeant North.

"Because I haven't been a child since the invaders came."

"That's the price you paid for surviving; we've all had to become someone else since they came."

"I can't remember what I was like before the invaders came. I can't recall ever having been anyone else but me."

Sergeant North took a swig out of a metal flask. Conrad was certain that whatever he was drinking, it was not water. After taking his drink, Sergeant North offered the flask to Conrad, who declined with a wave of his hand.

"So where are you going?" Conrad asked.

Sergeant North replied, "We have several storages of weapons and supplies hidden around here. The closest one is in my favorite direction."

"And that is?"

Sergeant North extended his right arm forward and pointed. "North."

"Of course it is. Also I'm pretty sure I saw an invader ship headed that way."

"Well, we're underneath the ground there and I don't care what anybody says, there's nothing to show that they can see beneath the ground, nothing."

"Right . . ."

Conrad had a strong suspicion that Sergeant North was not considered very bright in a pre-invader world. He decided he might as well get to know the other members of Sergeant North's unit. North gave him their names and the knowledge that they did not normally warm up to outsiders. One of the soldiers named Star was attending to Miracle, feeding him with ease. Conrad wondered if she had any children of her own, but decided not to ask that question. "Have you scored any major victories against the invaders lately?"

Star kissed Miracle's forehead as he gave a nice big yawn and fell asleep. Then she replied,

"Are you asking if we destroyed any of their ships or their settlements?"

"Settlements?"

"You haven't seen them? Then I guess hardly anyone has. The invaders always make sure that everyone is dead before they set up shop. But yeah, our cities and towns are theirs now. They're so confident of victory, they've already started colonizing."

Conrad suddenly remembered his childhood home. His family had left it to go into the city when the invaders arrived. It was supposed to have been safe there, but it was not. He wondered if his home still existed and if the invaders were living in it now. That idea sickened him.

"We're not going to let that happen, right? We're going to take our planet back and kill them all!"

Star sat up, took a few steps forward. Then she looked Conrad right in the eyes, "Even the children?"

Before Conrad could reply, Sergeant North cut in. "No one's ever seen an invader without its suit on. I don't even know what they look like. I don't know if they reproduce like us. Nevertheless, we have a right to wipe them all out, even their day-old young. No matter what happens, no matter if we win or lose, we have to kill as many of them as we can. If not to save us, then to give their next victims a fighting chance."

"I don't think we should stoop to their level," said Star.

Conrad butted in. "Can we just stop arguing and survive the day first?"

Sergeant North took out a pair of binoculars and took a long look ahead. "We are going to have to cross this canyon if we want to make it back before nightfall."

"There could be wild animals or invaders there," replied Conrad.

"Well, that's just a chance we are going to have to take," said Sergeant North.

Conrad sighed and looked at the rocky canyon. It was huge; if you went there without knowing where you were going you could get lost for days. There were plenty of gigantic rocks and boulders. Conrad knew an invader could be hiding behind any one of them. He noticed that the sun was setting with its red glow covering the land. It was blood red, a perfect reminder of all the violence that had happened today and all violence that would come tomorrow.

Conrad had a feeling that it was not over. He was sure that if Sergeant North's soldiers had killed the two invaders they would have returned by now. Sergeant North tapped his chin and he stood still for a few moments. He then pointed his index finger straight up and said, "I just got a feeling that we're not alone."

Lasers were suddenly coming from everywhere. Star and Conrad managed to take cover near a huge boulder while the invaders gunned down Sergeant North and the rest of his men. Miracle's cry pierced the air as Star handed him over to Conrad and returned fire. Conrad put his knees against his chest and gently rocked Miracle, trying to sooth him as much as he could.

They pinned us down and there's no getting out of this. If we run, they will shoot us dead; I can't do anything. No! I won't accept that! Miracle isn't dying today!

Conrad shouted, "Give me your laser rifle so I can charge at the invaders and draw their fire away. Then you and Miracle can escape.

"Conrad, that's crazy!"

"You need to live, Star, to take care of Miracle and carry on the fight. Me, I can die. I've lived enough of a life. Besides, no one's going to miss me."

"Conrad."

Star wanted to argue against everything that Conrad had just said, but found that she just could not. He was a stranger to her and she knew nothing of him. He gave her the baby while she gave him her blaster. Conrad gave Miracle a friendly pat on the head.

Then he rushed out from behind the rocks and fired at the invaders with everything he had. Lasers danced all around him. Still Conrad kept running to the left. He could not even see where he was going at this point; all he could do was fire his weapon. One hit and he was dead. That was the only thought flashing inside Conrad's mind. Conrad tripped over a pointy rock. Luckily, for him, he fell behind another huge boulder. He took this moment to stand up. He looked to the right and saw that his plan had worked. The invaders had focused all their fire on him, allowing Miracle and Star to escape.

Conrad did not expect that he could survive this, but he if could take one of those invaders out, that would be the ultimate victory. He fired at the outcrop where the invaders had taken cover. There was laser fire coming from all sides and he could not go anywhere. Conrad leaped on top of the boulder, saw an invader, and shot at its head. He missed and several laser blasters hit him square in the chest. He fell down on the ground with a thud, his mind free of all thought.

The smell of smoke woke Conrad up. His back hurt and the left side of his head was bleeding. Still, he was alive, but he could not stand up. Conrad soon realized that his wrists were bound together in some sort of sticky goo. No matter how hard he struggled, he could not break free. His eyes shot open and he saw eight invaders. Their helmets had retracted while they feasted on cooked meat. Conrad finally saw the face of his enemy for the first time. They were not the hideous monsters Conrad had pictured, but they still looked strange.

The invaders had white skin, except for two of them that had dark skin. They also had black, brown, or blond hair. Their eyes were different colors. Conrad's eyes, like all of his kind, were bright red and his skin a dark pink. He did not have a single hair on his body; but he had a tail, which was something that the invaders lacked. The invaders noticed that Conrad had awakened and they all pressed a hidden button on their left arms. The invader with blond hair crept over to Conrad.

Conrad inched away from the invader, but the invader stomped on his tail making Conrad unable to move. Conrad screeched in agony, while the blond haired invader gave a vile sneer. "You're not going anywhere you damn rat!"

Conrad found himself capable of understanding the invader's speech so he asked, "Rat? What's. . ?"

The blond haired invader kicked Conrad in his face. Some drops of blood leaked out of Conrad's nose as the invader shouted, "Rats are the closest thing to you where I come from. They are filthy disgusting animals that I enjoyed killing as a kid as much as I enjoy killing you vermin now!"

At that moment, Conrad's rage overcame his fear and he yanked his swollen tail free and got back up on his feet. "Is that why you came to Corth, just to slaughter us for the fun of it?"

The blond haired invader grabbed Conrad's shoulders and threw him back down to the ground. He gave Conrad a good kick in the ribs. "Sorry, I've been rude I should have introduced myself earlier. I am Major Samson and this is Unit 4. The reason we're all here is that we ran out of room back on planet Earth, so we took to the stars to find a new home. Sadly, when we landed here we discovered our new home already occupied. Thankfully that's being fixed every day."

Conrad wanted to kill Samson for saying that, but he knew that if he stood back up, Samson would just knock him down again. Samson ran his hands through his hair. "You're staying down this time, but I still see the fire in your eyes. It's just as strong as when we first met today."

"You . . ."

Samson kicked Conrad's groin while shouting, "That's right. I'm the invader that chased you all the way to that cliff. It spoiled my day, being denied the sight of you jumping off it with that whelp in yours arms!"

Conrad clenched his teeth together as he waited for the pain to pass. This invader had fired at him and Miracle for the thrill of it. For some reason, this did not surprise Conrad at all. Still, he needed to know. "Sergeant North sent men after you!"

"Yes, they killed my buddy. Then the rest of my unit swept in and chased them off. I know that bitch and brat escaped and you're going to tell me where they went off to."

"I honestly don't know and wouldn't tell you if I did. So you should just kill me."

Samson gave Conrad another hard kick in the groin and then a good kick in the face. Conrad spat out a mouthful of bloody saliva, while

Samson stepped on his tail again. "This is how it's going to work. I am going to hurt you until you tell me what I want to know. Then I'm going to keep hurting you until you beg me for death."

Samson forced Conrad back onto his feet and prepared to give him the beating of a lifetime. Conrad yanked his tail free and wrapped it around Samson's right ankle making him stumble onto the ground. Samson's own men snickered at him as he got back up and said, "Now you're going to get it!"

A laser blast came out of nowhere. The invaders had barely enough time to pick up their weapons, as the laser fire hailed on them. Conrad banged his bound wrists against a sharp rock to no avail. Samson picked up his laser rifle and fired several shots at a far off opponent, before aiming his rifle right at Conrad's head.

Conrad screamed and rammed Samson against a large rock. He kicked Samson repeatedly. He knew one of Samson's comrades could take him out with a single shot. He did not care. He was going to do everything in his power to put this monster down until he died. Samson fended off plenty of Conrad's kicks with his laser rifle. Conrad kicked the rifle out of Samson's hands and knocked it away with his tail. Still he could not damage Samson at all. His armor absorbed the impact of every kick. Samson pushed Conrad away and before either of them could strike another blow, the buzzing sound of laser guns surrounded them.

Conrad spun around and much to his delight and Samson's horror, all of Samson's comrades in arms were dead. The men Sergeant North had sent after Samson had returned with other Resistance members. Now sixteen Resistance fighters stood with Conrad. For the first time, even if it was for a moment, he felt safe. One of them shot the goo off Conrad's hands. Conrad rubbed his wrists. "Let me finish him off."

One of the Resistance members gave Conrad his rifle. Conrad aimed the gun right at Samson's chest. Samson laughed and shouted, "Do you think it makes any difference if you kill me? You're going to lose this war. Our numbers and technology are far greater than yours are. All you damn rats are going to die. Because you're all worthless mother. . !"

Conrad fired his laser rifle and Samson lived no more. Conrad had done it; he had killed an invader. Doing that no longer made them phantoms that haunted his nightmares, but creatures of blood and flesh like him. Despite what Samson had just uttered, Conrad knew they had a chance no matter how slim or unlikely it was. That was enough to make him stop running and start fighting back.

Matthew McKiernan lives in Yardley Pennsylvania. He has an MFA in creative writing from Rosemont College. He has published several science fiction and fantasy stories over the last few years.

Data Transfer
By Nick Morrison

"So, Alice. How are you feeling today?" Doctor Ko looked across her pristine white table at the less-than pristine woman sitting across from her.

Ratty hair framed a pale face thinned from stress. Eyes that darted at every surface around the room stared at Doctor Ko unfocused as the young woman said, "Well, there's a television playing in my brain and the Communists are coming to get us, so…"

It took a great deal of effort for Doctor Ko not to roll her eyes. The notion of Communism having been defeated over seventy-five years ago didn't apply to someone with Alice's addled mind. However, professionalism dictated that the good doctor go along with her patient's neuroses.

"Yes, but how do you feel?"

Alice wrapped bony arms around herself. She was wearing white and the room and everything in it being white gave the impression that Alice was simply a part of the furniture that had decided to become sentient; albeit with mental problems that had no right to plague her in the first place.

"Um, okay I guess."

Doctor Ko smiled. "Fantastic!" A wave of her hand over the smooth, epicurean surface of her desk brought up the holographic image of Alice's medical charts. "You've responded well to the drug treatments. Are you still seeing the, er...Faceless Fiend everywhere?"

In spite of her promise to herself to remain professional, Doctor Ko couldn't help but grin. It was such a ridiculous thing, after all: people like Alice were few and far between given the advancement in medical sciences since the turn of the millennium. If it weren't for conclusive brain scans, Doctor Ko would think that her patient was simply faking her schizophrenia for attention. It wasn't as though most people would take notice of a woman as workaday as Alice on the streets of New Washington.

Or in the corridors of Saggitarius-6, the station currently orbiting around Kepler 22b.

Something like annoyance flickered on Alice's face for a moment. "No," she said. "Not since I came here."

"Well, that's good to hear." Especially seeing as how, in her first weeks in Sagittarius's medical bay, Alice had given the security detail a run for their money by claiming that she could see her Faceless Fiend in every surface of the corridor walls.

A pleasant voice with a gentle Irish brogue sounded in the room. "Time is fifteen hundred, thirty-six. Weather report for major Kepler cities: New Manhattan, twenty-two degrees Celsius; New Houston, thirty-seven degrees Celsius; New Calgary, eighteen degrees Celsius with a chance of snow. Sagittarius news—

"Oh!" Alice shrunk inward on herself, as if that were somehow still possible. She clapped her hands over her ears. Doctor Ko frowned, and with another wave of her hand, collapsed the hologram containing her patient's information.

"Alice, please," she said, getting to her feet and going to the refreshment station by the emerald green projection of a ficus plant, "you've

179

heard Papa's announcements for the past six weeks."

"I don't understand how it works," Alice said, sounding on the verge of tears. "It's a voice that comes out of nowhere that sounds different every day. And it talks to people as if it's a human—

"That's because," Doctor Ko said with the patience of a mother addressing a precocious toddler, "Papa has a personality core." A stream of jet-black coffee, a rare commodity granted to Sagittarius 6 by the government back on Kepler, streamed out of the refreshment dispenser. A moment later, cream and sugar shot into the mug in Doctor Ko's hand. "Mmm," the doctor said after a much-needed drink, "that's good."

She returned to her desk. With caffeine now flowing through her, she felt more capable of addressing Alice in a matter befitting a doctor. "We've been through this with your cognitive behavioural therapy," she said. "There's nothing to fear from Papa; he's just a highly advanced computer program."

But Alice seemed inconsolable. Doctor Ko had to admit that it must not have been easy for the poor woman: everything was a threat to someone with Alice's illness. Frankly it was a miracle that she'd made it to Sagittarius 6 before something drastic had happened back on the planet now spinning below them.

Doctor Ko sighed. "What would make you feel better, Alice?"

"Get it out," Alice said, half-sobbing. Her fingers were snaked in her own sere, mousey hair.

"You know I can't do that, Alice. Here, if it'll make you feel better..." Doctor Ko drew up the holographic screen of her personal computer. She flicked through her personal files until she found the schematics for the technology that controlled Papa.

"Papa is just a computer," she reminded her unfortunate patient. "During construction, a very famous scientist by the name of Randall Katz uploaded his personality via data transfer—I'm sure you know all about that. It's how we still have movie stars from fifty years ago."

Alice stared at the screen and Doctor Ko through her fingers; judging by how wide her eyes were, the doctor knew she had the woman's attention.

"The only difference between Papa and Angelina Jolie is that Papa is a computer system hardwired through all of Sagittarius 6, and Angie is just an simulacrum with a dead movie star's personality and talent installed. We have a scientist's intelligence and persona; Kepler has the actual man, still living and breathing and being smart as ever. Just with not as much intelligence as he used to possess."

Papa controlled everything on the station, from hourly announcements to the security system. Doctor Ko and the other residents had lucked out when Professor Katz had transferred not only his intelligence, but his benevolent personality into the computer systems on the station. It had been a sacrifice on the man's part, but Katz had loved science enough to give up some of what made him who he was for the field.

For a moment, Alice continued to stare at the holographic screen. There was something in her normally alert and frightened eyes that pleased Doctor Ko—a sort of intense focus that she hadn't seen there before.

Smiling, the doctor said, "How does that make you feel?"

Slowly, Alice dropped her hands to her lap. The she smiled, a gesture that made her look at least ten years younger. "Good," she said, her voice stronger and more confident than Doctor Ko had heard it in six weeks. "Very, very good."

#

It only took Alice a week to get into the control room. In that time, she forgot about the incessant fear that she would once again mistake her racing thoughts for voices; she forgot about the fear that she would once again see the Faceless Fiend leering at her from behind the walls of the space station.

And she became completely transfixed with the lilting voice of Papa.

During her evening walks, in which the only thing that supervised her was the watchful gaze of the security systems, she followed his voice. Eventually, Alice was able to peg that the control room was located down the corridor in the East wing where the technology staff was housed.

Under the watchful eye of Doctor Ko, she took her nightly sleeping pill and anti-psychotic medication. Only, when the doctor turned to leave the room, Alice bit the sleeping pill in half, and stashed the remainder under her bamboo pillow.

Her determination to see Papa, to be in that room, carried her through the worst of the anxiety that lingered in the wake of her weeks long treatment. It allowed her to sneak out of her room in the middle of the night and give the men and women in the East wing a drink from her contraband bottle of iced tea.

One by one, they nodded off at their workstations. Alice pegged it down to a combination of late hours and the bits of sleeping pill she'd stirred into the beverage she'd served them.

Now, with hands trembling, Alice took the key card from the lead worker and found her way to the nearly unobtrusive panel of wall where she'd determined that the computer controlling Papa lay.

The control room was a dark, lit only by the machines that paneled the walls, and the massive computer in the middle. An immense glowing sphere hovered over this computer, glowing faintly blue, and then green, and then yellow.

Alice felt cold with excitement as she drew nearer and nearer the computer. This was it; this was where the professor had uploaded his personality and intelligence—the very essence of who he was. She'd gleaned as much information as she could from the staff of Sagittarius, all of whom were only too willing to tell her the truth if it meant ridding them of a patient whose histrionics had became all too tiring over the last month and a bit.

It took Alice only a moment to find what she sought—two suction cups that attached to the temples. A long wire connected the headpiece to the machine below Papa's intelligence cortex.

Just before she attached the cups to the sides of her head, Alice felt a fleeting moment of panic. She'd lived with this maddening disease since the age of twenty-four. And while it had driven her to terror time and time again, the thought of suddenly finding herself without it was all the more terrifying because it was change; change was to venture forth into the unknown and science only knew what was waiting on the other side.

An all too familiar feeling stole over her, constricting the air in her lungs and making her keenly, uncomfortably aware of her heartbeat. Her thoughts became a tangled mess as words and ideas tumbled over one another.

I can focus, she made herself think. I am in control. Control. Con. Trol. A mole. The goal. Pole. North Pole. Cold. Winter. Snow. Go. Toe.

No. Alice pictured a stop signal, the kind she'd seen when she'd still had her feet on the solid ground of the planet below. It was a technique she'd taught herself when she'd been more lucid. Though her mind thought that there was danger, though it invented and created threats in a sadistic effort to keep her safe, there were certain things that were ingrained into the human brain. And one them was a red signal for halting any and all activity.

Opening her eyes, Alice looked at the machine in front of her. She kept the stop signal at the forefront of her mind until the incessant noises in her ears began to dull to a quiet sotto voce.

The red signal in her mind's eye turned green.

Go.

Alice attached the suction cups to her temples, switched on the machine in front of her, and waited for the sweet oblivion of whatever would happen next.

#

Doctor Ko hated it when things didn't go as they ought. In this day and age of superior technology, there was no room for malfunction or being waylaid. Therefore, when the air lock to Sagittarius 6 didn't immediately open for her after scanning her identification card twice, she was, to put it lightly, mildly perturbed. Of course, the retinal and hand scanners had been installed for such an occasion, and there was the voice recognition core installed in Papa that was meant to work under extreme circumstances. But why the devil couldn't the first point of entry have worked the way it was supposed to?

Sighing, Doctor Ko pressed her hand on the gel panel, trying to ignore the slimy, cool feeling of the surface. There was brief pulse of heat as the scan activated, and Doctor Ko was just thinking that she'd have to have word with the programming staff once she made it to her office, when a loud siren filled the air lock and a red light flashed.

"What the hell?" Doctor Ko stared at the orbital camera in front of the air lock. "Papa!" She cried. "What's going on?"

"Access denied." Papa's voice, so like that of the man he'd been in life, was somehow louder than the sirens blaring in Doctor Ko's ears.

Fuming, Doctor Ko stooped to use the optical scanner. She was only a fraction of an inch away from the device when the miniscule shutters slid over the lens, shielding it from view.

"Papa!" Doctor Ko made sure to raise her voice, hoping that the vocal recognition would pick it up over the sirens.

"Access denied. We don't let the Reds in."

Doctor Ko frowned. She stood on tiptoe, peering through the portal window in the airlock. She could just see the corridor beyond, devoid of people. Even for this hour, that was unusual. The orderlies worked around the clock, and Doctor Ko knew that there were at least three or four patients who enjoyed going for a stroll through the station.

"Open the door, Papa," Doctor Ko said. She banged on the portal window, as if hoping that it would give way.

"Access denied. We don't let the Reds in," Papa repeated. The cacophony of noise and the glaring flash of the red lights began to wear at Doctor Ko's nerves. She pushed against the airlock. "We know who you're working for. The Faceless Fiend isn't going to get in. In to win. Win. Sin. Sinners go to Hell."

Doctor Ko whirled around and stared at the emotionless camera on the ceiling. She'd heard that kind of phrase before. Only it hadn't come from Papa.

It had come from Alice during her early days at Sagittarius 6.

"Papa..."

"Nobody home." Papa's voice, smooth as silk. "Not letting you in. In and out, in and out, the bear is tearing his teeth through the trout."

Trying hard not to give into the blind panic rising in her throat, Doctor Ko stared through the portal window once more. This time she could see somebody walking down the corridor--somebody in loose fitting white clothes, with dirty blonde hair.

The alarm was almost deafening; the lights, blinding. Doctor Ko couldn't think, couldn't focus. She banged her hands against the portal window to the attention of the lone figure.

Alice stopped, and turned to face the airlock door. For the first time in six weeks, Doctor Ko saw an acuity and lucidity in her patient's gaze. And there was something more, something cruel and vindictive like a cat that had cornered a terrified mouse.

"Alice!" Doctor Ko screamed. "Alice, let me in!"

But Alice only smiled, tapped the sides of her head and said, "Feeling better now, doctor. I don't think we need you anymore. Do we, Papa?"

"We don't let the Reds in," Papa said, still with that chipper, accented voice.

"Please!" Doctor Ko screamed. "He'll activate the elimination procedure and he'll—he'll kill me!"

Alice walked towards the portal window. "And tell me doctor: how does that make you feel?"

Nick Morrison is a native of Canada. He holds a journalism degree, and divides his time between British Columbia and Alberta. Data Transfer is his first published work.

Twitter: @TheWordFerret
Blog: https://thewordferret.wordpress.com/

Hero's End
By John Haas

"... join us on Inside the Hero as we continue our special series on Canada's own super team, the Northern Protectors. Tonight on episode three we follow the Grim Ghost and sidekick Phantom Boy as they patrol the streets of Calgary. "Ghost, as most people call him, has agreed to allow us to document his nightly adventures for one week just as fellow heroes Canadian Shield and Ricochet have."

A string of face shots fills the screen showing all thirteen members of the Northern Protectors. The shots shrink into a map of Canada, each hero's picture going to their respective province or territory. The camera zooms in on Alberta and a picture of the Grim Ghost.

"Clad in black from head to foot the hero conceals his face under a full mask. On his chest the famous insignia of two spectral green eyes in a hazy fog. No flowing cape, no flashy ornaments or decorations—everything about the man is sleek and dangerous. The only addition to his

costume the paralyzing-gas gun that has become his calling card.

True to his nature Ghost is all business and straight to the point."

"Keep up, and stay out of the way." Ghost says looking at the camera. "This isn't a game."

"Ghost has informed us we are investigating his old enemy, Chinook, tonight." The camera cuts to an exterior shot of a wide warehouse, a closed loading bay door in the front. *"The villain has been preparing an unknown scheme inside this nondescript building."* Ghost and Phantom Boy stalk toward a smaller man door on the side.

"Chinook is the type of villain who pops up in Ghost's life from time to time, always trying to prove himself a major threat and join the likes of Mindshriek and White Fang in reputation. In reality he is more nuisance than true danger."

Inside, Ghost heads forward, the camera following him, while Phantom Boy heads into the darkness on the right.

"Why...?" The interviewer starts.

Ghost raises his hand in a warning.

The camera switches to a green night-vision view and everything is more visible in the dim warehouse. It follows Ghost around stacks of boxes and pallets until coming to an open area. A wind howls through the warehouse, pushing Ghost and camera crew backward.

"Did you think I wasn't aware of you coming?" A hollow voice taunts from the darkness.

The camera pushes forward and bumps into the back of Ghost. The hero waves them back.

"And you brought friends for me to play with. How nice."A beam flashes out of the darkness.

The Grim Ghost seems about to dodge, then looks over his shoulder at the camera crew. He stands taller, blocking the screen of the camera. The wind picks up as the beam hits Ghost and lifts the hero from the floor. He is buffeted back and forth against the metal warehouse racks. Across the open space a scuffle is heard. The camera refocuses on where the beam came from. As quick as it began, the wind dies and Ghost falls twenty feet to the ground where he lies unmoving.

"Ghost?" The interviewer says from off screen.

"A moment later Phantom Boy comes out of the darkness dragging the unconscious and handcuffed form of Chinook. A confident smile covers the young boy's face until he sees his mentor."

"Ghost...?" Phantom Boy drops Chinook and runs to the fallen hero. "No..."

#

Erik Cromwell woke in a hospital room and lay still, taking in his surroundings, getting his bearings. The head of his bed was raised enough for him to look around. Light from the bathroom shone into the room, giving some illumination to see by. A beige couch sat on his right, in front of a wide, clean window. Outside, a night-time view of an unfamiliar street.

The room was clean and quiet, but with a vague antiseptic smell that made Erik think of death and last hope. An IV on his right snaked its way down to a vein in the back of his hand.

"Brought down by Chinook, and on TV too," he sighed. "Couldn't have been White Fang." But White Fang was insane, if it had been him they would all be dead.

Still groggy, his hand reached up and touched his face, no mask; so he was here under his secret identity. He wondered what story Alex had given. Erik tried to force himself into a sitting position and found his arms and legs weak, unresponsive. How badly had he been hurt? With a groan he flopped back and eyed the call button but decided against it. Until he saw his wife, Maddy, or his son he didn't know what to tell anyone. He could blow his secret identity with a couple of words.

Maddy would be here tomorrow. He was surprised she wasn't here now, waiting for him to wake up. Last time she wouldn't leave... Last time. Inner calm drained from him in an instant.

"The last time? No."

Only one time had he ended up in a hospital like this, the time Chinook had gotten the drop on him while he protected the documentary crew. He remembered that stay in the hospital and the day he'd been discharged, remembered Maddy taking him home.

"Then, why am I here?" Had he been injured in battle? Erik leaned his head back into the pillow and closed his eyes, cutting off visual input. "What's the last thing I remember?"

Fuzzy, elusive memories spiralled inside his head. Le Destin's latest scheme... something with clones. Entropy and The Void, two maniacs doing their best to bring about the end of everything. Fighting the Evil Legion beside the other Protectors. Yes, that he remembered. Other memories came and went in a blur but nothing to reveal how he had gotten here.

What was wrong with his head? Why couldn't he think? His eyes strayed to the IV bag and the line that came down to his hand. "Is that it? Am I drugged?" He considered the needle in the back of his hand for a long time then shook his head.

The bedside table had a lamp but no telephone. "I need to talk to Maddy."

Aching, weak muscles screamed with effort as he forced his legs to the side of the bed. He rolled to his left and stopped. Erik swept the sheet aside and stared in horror at the bony, atrophied legs inside his pyjama pants.

"My God, how long have I been here?" He rolled back and held thin hands up in front of his face. Dehydration, malnourishment—that would explain the weakness. He gave his fists experimental squeezes, they felt tight and stiff, like too little skin across too much bone.

To his left the door made a soft sighing noise. He flopped back against his pillow, pulling the sheet over his legs. His eyes drew down to a bare squint which would look closed. That brief movement had taken more out of him than he thought possible and he fought to bring his breathing back to normal.

A nurse entered and made her way across the room, a small light in her hand playing across the bed. He could jump up, overpower her and demand answers. But would he be terrorizing an innocent nurse? Would she be able to overpower *him* or call out an alarm? Better to play asleep.

"How are you doing tonight?" She asked.

Erik forced himself to breathe normally.

"Hmm, looks like you've been moving a bit. That's good." She adjusted his sheet, pulling it further up his chest. "That would explain the bed alarm." She made a note on a clipboard. "If you don't wake up soon though, I'll have to fit you with a catheter."

For the next ten minutes she set about doing tasks – changing his IV bag, closing the blinds – all the time chatting away to Erik without giving any useful information. When she left he opened his eyes and lay still in the semi-darkness, thinking.

Everything seemed authentic, but he'd been trapped by too many mad doctors to take anything at face value. Every instinct told him something was off here, not the way it should be, and his instincts kept him alive.

"Okay, what *do* I know?" He held up his forefinger. "If I've been hurt then Maddy would be waiting here. So..." Second finger. "She doesn't know where I am. Someone else brought me here." Yes, but who? Friend or enemy? "No way to know, not yet."

Third finger. "My mask is gone, so whoever it was knows my face." Erik thought for long moments, looking at the unfamiliar fingers pointing toward the ceiling. Fourth finger. "I've been here a while, a month at the least. God, Maddy, what you must be thinking."

He needed to contact her, let her know he was alive.

Fifth finger. "I can't trust anyone here, not until I know what's going on." He reached over and pulled the IV out of the back of his hand. The bed sheet pressed against the wound for a couple of minutes would stop any bleeding.

"Now, what did that nurse say about a bed alarm?" He looked around, seeing nothing that could fit the description. His free hand ran over the sheets and found the outline of a pad underneath him. He nodded; remove the weight and a nurse comes.

"So how do I beat it?"

Erik confirmed the bleeding on his hand had stopped, then rolled his body to the side again. While he waited for the nurse to return he traced the outline of the pad under him until the electrical cord was found, then followed it to a box that sat beside the mattress. An on-off switch at the top of the box allowed him a brief smile. He eased himself back, hoping he appeared as he had a few minutes ago. The door opened again and his smile vanished with the realization he had made one mistake.

The same nurse took a step into the room and glanced toward him. "Damned alarm." she muttered and left. He was lucky. If she had come any closer she would have seen the IV was out. As the door closed he reached over and grabbed the box, feeling along it, looking for the switch and flipping it to the off position.

The nurse would be calling someone about the faulty alarm soon, or maybe getting a replacement pad. In either case he had limited time. His feet hit the ground, and his body came close to following. The bedside table stopped his fall and supported him until he could stand on his own. Erik looked at his legs, felt the weakness, and knew he'd been there much longer than a month. Pins and needles assaulted his legs as he shuffled across the room, headed for the door.

Where could he find a phone? Another room? No, he couldn't count on having the time to search. He had to get out.

Feeling came to his legs with a painful throb as he swerved toward the closet. "Too slow. Faster, damn it. Move your ass, Erik." There would only be this one chance.

Inside the closet were a pair of blue slippers and a thin coat. They would have to do, better than nothing, at least. He grabbed the coat and jammed his feet into the slippers, then turned and headed for the entry door, moving quicker now.

The hallway outside the room was empty and quiet, the deep silence of late night. Without another thought Erik headed down the corridor toward the nearest stairwell, using the wall for support. At the door to the stairs he glanced behind him; no nurse yet but it wouldn't be long. He turned and climbed down the stairs at the quickest pace he could manage. A small amount of strength and stamina had returned but they were dwindling commodities that needed to be rationed.

Before entering the lobby he took a moment to get the coat on. An empty security desk sat in the center of the lobby, a newspaper and cup of coffee waiting for the guard's return.

"And that's why the heroes always win."

#

Erik headed straight for the exit, two doors with a small vestibule between them. Outside the first door he could already feel the cold night air outside, could hear the steady wind. He would need to move fast once he got out there.

"But, which way do I go?"

To his right he caught movement and tensed for an attack. Whirling toward it he found himself ready to fight a reflection. A long mirror covered one side of the vestibule. Relief started to wash into him, then he *really* saw the reflection.

"What the hell?" He stepped toward the mirror and reached out as if touching it would change what he saw. In the mirror stared back the grizzled face of a stranger. The hair was thin and discoloured; eyes close together and sunken. "Who...?"

It wasn't his body.

All the puzzle pieces came together. "The body is the real trap, not the hospital." Someone had stuck Erik in this frail, weak body and left him to die.

Mindshriek. It had to be him. Master of dreams, illusions and false memories. "But why...? No, think about that later."

Now Erik knew for certain he had to get out of there, get somewhere safe. He pushed the outer door and headed into the night. The air hit him like a cold fist, he could feel it deep in the bones of the body he was riding the moment he stepped onto the sidewalk. No warm Calgary Chinook passing through tonight. Judging by the temperature and the lack of snow on the ground it had to be November or December.

A quick look over his shoulder told him no one was following. He picked a direction and looked at the convalescent home—Mercy House—

while walking away from it. They had stuck him in a real facility? But, why? Unless...

"I was never supposed to wake up, was I?"

Behind it, in the distance, was the Peter Lougheed Hospital. With that landmark he had an idea of where he was. A station for the C-train—Calgary's light rail transit system—would be up the street, a quick walk. In short time he would be away. If he could make it downtown he could get to one of his safe houses.

And, there would be a pay phone at the station.

By the time he reached the corner he had started to question how quick a walk it would be. In the parking lot of a Mac's he rested, his heart pounding inside his chest while the cold air wheezed through his teeth. Waiting. Waiting. The cold pressed against him like a second skin.

"Why didn't they kill me?" He wheezed. "Why play with me like this?" It didn't make sense. He would make them regret it.

Going home was out of the question now, even though he worried for Maddy. It was probable that whoever had done this knew Erik Cromwell was the Grim Ghost. Home is the first place they would look for him.

Headlights pulled into the parking lot and Erik forced himself to his feet. Wind blew past, biting at his exposed ankles and cutting through his thin clothing. He crossed 36th Street and took the shorter route of heading up the tracks to the platform.

Air wheezed into his lungs and huffed back out. One step at a time. Though everything in him screamed to hurry he went at a speed the body could handle, knowing that if it collapsed he would never get where he was going.

Erik frowned, his brain turning things over as he walked. "Mindshriek doesn't repeat himself." The Northern Protectors had fought him for years and this felt like the time the villain had transferred five of the Protectors into their enemies' bodies.

"What am I missing?" Could it be someone else? The Grim Ghost had enough villains to choose from, but did any of them have the ability?

"Something else." Something about that time Mindshriek had switched them with their enemies, a long time ago, the way they had beaten him... "Madcap's machine." He snapped his fingers.

Madcap had been a one-shot villain who did his time and reformed, but he had one real claim to fame: The Machine. A mechanism that cancelled out the effects of all other machines. That day Vixen, one of the other villains, had mentioned the machine, dropping the careless comment, but Erik saw the look in her eyes. "She always did have a thing for Shield."

"Madcap`s machine cancelled out Mindshriek's once; it can do it again." And it was in the trophy room at Hero's End.

Hero's End. The splashy comic-book name for the Northern Protectors' base of operations— Meeting hall, monitors, training room, trophy room. Canadian Shield, always in love with the image of the superhero, had built it on a man-made island on Lake Ontario just outside Toronto.

Next stop, the safe house for his spare costume, gas gun and the transporter to Hero's End. "Hold on Maddy, I'm coming."

The C-Train's honour system saved him. He would be able to get on to a train even though he had no money. But was the train still running?

The hard metal bench on the Rundle station platform was cold through his thin pants but still a welcome rest after the walking. Inside the glass enclosure Erik was cold, but at least he was out of the wind. In a moment, when he caught his breath, he would go look for that pay phone.

His eyes had started to close when the sound of a footstep to his right alerted him. He looked over at a man standing at the edge of the platform, looking up the tracks. So the train *was* still running. The man made a point of staying far away from Erik.

"Ghost." The man said.

Erik spun his head toward this man who knew his identity, only the man wasn't even looking at him. A sleek black aircraft, near silent, came toward them, passing over Sunridge Mall. The design was Erik's, more sleek and futuristic, quieter, but still his. The logo of two green eyes in a circle of darkness on the side of the craft convinced him. It was the Ghostship.

Erik watched as the vehicle sped past him, headed in the direction of Mercy House. So they hadn't only trapped him in the body, they'd stolen his life too—his life as the Ghost at least. Would they have assumed his Erik Cromwell identity too?

"No. Alex and Maddy wouldn't be fooled by that, not for long." When they realized it wasn't him they would contact the Northern Protectors. Would that be a mistake though? What about the other Protectors? Had they been taken over too?

He couldn't phone home, not yet.

A shape dropped from the craft a few blocks over as the ship hovered, both silhouetted against the bright moon. They knew he was missing. The hunt had begun.

The train arrived and he hurried on, grateful for the warmth inside. He sat in the empty car and watched out the window as the Ghostship turned away from the home, searching, a shadowed figure holding onto the ship's ladder as it went. Whoever had taken his life had made improvements to the vehicle. The ship was so much closer to silent, something he'd been striving for. He would have to take that engine apart and learn how it was done, once he reclaimed his life. With that ship he could be at Hero's End in minutes, even though it was halfway across the country.

Then it was out of sight and Erik was on his way downtown. The trip on the C-train gave him time to recuperate his energy. Once he made it to the safe house...

Surely, the imposter couldn't know where that was.

#

Erik stood on the far side of the street, watching his safe house until he was satisfied it was empty. His fingers and toes hurt to move and he was afraid of hypothermia and frostbite. Much longer on the street and this body would collapse, either from fatigue or cold. He needed to get inside, now. Erik leaned against the dirty red bricks and closed his eyes for a moment, gathering the energy to move, then forced himself to cross the street and get around back. A small keypad hung to the right of the heavy metal door. Freezing fingers punched in the code and he was rewarded with the sound of metal scraping against metal as the door unlocked for him. Inside, the open area of the empty store was somewhat warmer than the air outside.

In the middle of the room he pulled on a floorboard and entered another lengthy code into the keypad hidden underneath. A hesitation, then the mechanism turned. A stairway opened three feet away and Erik rushed forward.

At the bottom of the stairs he collapsed against the wall and looked around at the small heated room, waiting for feeling to return to his fingers and toes. Costume, computer, first aid kit. Someone had been here, he could tell, though not recently.

"They do know about the safe house then," he muttered.

No time to rest. His spare costume hung on the far side of the room in a glass display case. The clothing would solve two problems: The thermal fabric would keep him warm, and the strength augmenting exoskeleton would help his weak muscles.

Erik opened the cabinet and, struggling with cold, fumbling fingers, dressed in his costume. The gas gun was a comfort on his hip, even though it only had one charge. The shell of the costume gave his body an immediate, much needed boost of strength and the battery pack powering it was full.

Though the costume didn't quite fit his strange new body he stood taller, more confident, stronger. "I am the Grim Ghost, and the villain responsible will pay."

Once dressed, the Grim Ghost opened the compartment at the bottom of the cabinet and was rewarded with the sight of his emergency transporter. A small, hand-held apparatus that each one of the Northern Protectors had as a backup to bring them to Hero's End. He tucked it into his belt.

Next was contacting Canadian Shield though he should get the hell out of there. "James would check on me though."

The computer booted up and he entered his password. Slow, but he was happy for the chance to rest while the suit did its job of warming him. He punched in the number from memory then clicked dial and held his breath.

"Hello." A woman's face filled the screen and looked at him. "Erik?"

He hit end and headed for the stairs. The costume loaned him vitality but he couldn't overdo it, short bursts would be best. In the alley behind the safe house he stopped and gripped the transporter.

Vixen! The woman who answered the phone was Shield's old enemy, Vixen. Now he *knew* everyone was in trouble. If he and Shield had been compromised then Earthquake, Fleur-De-Lis and the rest of the Protectors would be too.

"Now what? Have they taken Hero's End too?" Probably. "What else can I do?"

No answer so he held the transporter in front of him and gripped it tight in one fist. He wasn't a fan of travelling this way. His thumb stabbed at the button and the feeling of being pulled sideways assailed him. The alley behind the safe house shimmered, replaced by the inside of the white landing room at Hero's End.

#

"Welcome Grim Ghost."

The Ghost crouched at the sound of the voice before remembering the computer that greeted all of them on arrival. The element of surprise would be gone now, but with luck anyone who heard will think he was the imposter. He stepped forward and through the doorway, creeping his way down the corridor that would take him to the trophy room. It seemed that the place was empty.

The monitor room was ahead on his left. Stealthy, quiet, he crept to the room and peered around the corner. A huge man dressed all in red sat motionless in the seat, staring at the bank of monitors that showed what was happening in the country.

"Red Oak," he whispered.

The massive hero from P.E.I. rocked in the chair which he dwarfed. Was it possible that only he and Shield had been targeted after all? He couldn't take the chance, this was the one chance he would get and someone in Red Oak's body could tear him apart.

Ghost aimed his gas gun at the back of the man in red and pulled the trigger. An explosion of gas and sandy particles encircled the man who stiffened in his chair. Coming closer Ghost looked into the eyes of the man behind the red mask.

"You're not Red Oak. Who are you really?"

The huge man made no sound, just stared at Ghost with piercing eyes.

"My Red Oak would know this, you'll be paralyzed for the next twenty minutes."

Ghost turned and headed to the trophy room, a wide, tall room housing memorabilia from their years of adventures. A long stairway led to a circular walk above for a bird's eye view of the trophies. Ghost glanced up at the stars visible through the clear glass dome. How many times had he entered and exited through the door there instead of using the transporter?

A giant gong, the Digger's drills, one of Atomicon's robots, a seemingly innocent child's doll under a thick glass dome... but where had the giant totem pole come from? Or the glowing golden book that hovered inside a cage of energy?

"Where is Madcap's Machine?" He had twenty minutes to find it... more like fifteen now. The Grim Ghost waded through rows of trophies, items familiar and unfamiliar. Just as the layout started to seem right and he was sure it was around the next corner it changed again.

"Come on, Ghost, come on." Row after row until he was passing by things he had already seen. Ten minutes left.

Ghost leaned against the display of the Thinker's assorted eyeglasses. He stared at them for a full minute before realizing what he was looking at. No time for subtlety, he put his fist through the glass of the display cabinet and grabbed the third pair inside. A tag which said: Locating Glasses, fluttered to the ground.

He jammed the glasses on his head. "Madcap's Machine." He said, turning in a slow circle until a glowing shape popped up in the distance. "Yes."

Ghost headed across the trophy room and smashed another cabinet. How had he missed this one? He reached through the glass and lifted out Madcap's Machine with care.

"Dad."

The Ghost spun and saw the imposter who had stolen his identity, close up for the first time, standing in the doorway of the trophy room, not ten feet away. It wasn't Mindshriek. This was a large man, more than six feet tall, he wore a futuristic version of the Ghost costume, looking more like a hard rubber armour. Ghost looked up at the glass dome and could see the outline of the Ghostship hovering above.

What was it the imposter had said? Ghost held Madcap's Machine in his right hand, thumb over the activator switch.

"Dad, no." The other man held his hands out. "Don't do it. It sets off an E.M.P."

Dad? Is *that* what he had heard? "Who are you?"

"Dad, it's me." The other Grim Ghost swept off the rubber mask and dropped it to the ground, making no effort to come closer. The face *was* familiar. Was it possible?

"Dad," the man repeated, slower. "It's me. Alex."

"Alex?"

"Yes, Dad. I was so worried about you."

The fog that packed his brain lifted. Was this his son? Impossible. Alex was a kid, his sidekick. Alex took a step toward him and stopped, concern obvious on his face.

"No, it's a trick." Ghost backed toward the winding stairs. "Stay away from me." He turned and ran up the stairs to the walkway and the dome.

"Dad," the voice called after him.

He slammed through the door to the outside and stopped, his short burst of energy finished. Memories buffeted him from all sides, things that couldn't be true. The Ghostship hovered with its ladder down, the young worried face of a Phantom Boy inside the cockpit.

"My son," the man said from behind him. "He's been Phantom Boy for two weeks now."

Ghost spun back and looked at the other man.

"Dad, we have to get you back."

What was it? Had he jumped into the future? Alternate reality? Something had sent his son and grandson from the future? All things that Madcap's Machine would solve.

He slammed his thumb down on the contact button. A sphere of energy shot out from the machine, engulfing everything for hundreds of feet.

Nothing happened. He was still stuck in the old, infirm body and looking at the other Ghost he knew, it was all true. Fragmented memories returned, filling in some holes but leaving others confusing and vague.

"Alex?" he said wearily.

"Yes, Dad"

He dropped Madcap's Machine. His muscles ached again and he discovered the machine had only succeeded in destroying his own exoskeleton. He was back to using his own muscles.

"Dad, we have to get you back," Alex repeated.

There was no scheme by Mindshriek or any other villain, no body switch. Things fell into place in his mind and the answer was much worse. His gut felt like he'd been punched. "Why? So I can lie in a hospital bed waiting for death?"

Alex stood still. "You do remember?"

Erik shook his head. "Not really. A little. I'm filling in some blanks on my own."

Alex let out a long sigh. "You started having episodes two years ago. Forgetfulness at first. Then regression. You'd been long retired by then. It went downhill pretty quick. These days you're in and out of being comatose."

The Ghostship gave a little whine and turned.

Erik thought about Maddy, something his mind shied away from. "I... I tried to call Shield."

"I know. Tracey—Vixen—called me and told me where the call had come from. We were still searching near the home."

"So, Vixen and Shield?"

Alex smiled. "Yep, he finally reformed her. They married years ago." He hesitated a moment. "You were the best man."

Something in that seemed familiar. "Oh... Good for them." A pause. Erik glanced at the Ghostship as it drifted back then came forward again. "What happened to the Evil Legion?"

"The one you knew is gone. Manitou is dead, Jack in the Box retired and runs a pawn shop. The others have been replaced by their children."

"Life goes on." Erik rested his hand on the butt of his gas gun. "Did we make any difference at all? All those battles?"

"Of course you did, Dad. You protected Canada."

"Dad!" The speaker on the ship wailed. "I can't control the ship. It's..." The Ghost ship wobbled from side to side then spun to the right.

"The ship must have been on the outskirts of the effect." Alex said. "Dad, I'm paralyzed. My costume..."

Erik looked at Alex and saw his son struggling inside the frozen suit.

"Save my son, Dad."

No time for thought, Erik turned and jumped for the ladder of the Ghostship. Unfamiliar muscles and dead exoskeleton, he came close to missing, grabbing onto the bottom rungs.

"My communicator will still work, it's shielded." Alex called to him.

Erik had no idea what Alex was talking about but he forced his way up the ladder. Hand. Foot. Hand. Foot. The longest climb of his life until he could force himself inside of the Ghostship as it weaved side to side. Flopping his body onto the floor, all he wanted to do was collapse and sleep, instead he got his feet under him and made his way forward, holding on to the equipment as he went for balance. In the cockpit he saw the wild eyed fear in the face of his grandson and felt the shame of knowing he had caused it.

"Grampa." Phantom Boy said.

Erik sank into the other chair. "Yes, and you're my grandson...Um..."

"Erik, just like you."

He smiled at the homage. "Right. Erik, is there any way to land this thing?"

His grandson shrugged.

"No." The voice came over the radio. Alex. "There's a time warp delay around the ship that let's everything happen slower but that ship is going down."

Erik turned toward his grandson. "Your dad is a fine man, follow his lead in battle and you'll do fine," he hit the eject button that flung the younger Erik out of the ship.

"Get out of there, Dad."

Erik watched out the cockpit window at where the ship was headed. All he saw were buildings and city streets in the distance. Straight into the heart of Toronto. "Can't, Alex."

"Dad!"

Erik pulled back on the controls, trying to get the ship to swerve from its course. "I always thought I would die in battle with Johnny Fatal or Stonewall, not in a hospital bed from too many hits to the skull."

"There's new treatments. New drugs."

"Do they work?" he grunted.

The ship responded, ever so slightly. A degree to the left.

"I... No, not yet."

Turning. Turning.

"You're doing it Dad, the ship is turning."

The question he'd been avoiding. It was time. "What about your mom? Where's Maddy?"

He could see a strip of water now to the side of the cockpit window.

"Mom passed away three years ago, just before you started having the... episodes."

He felt the truth of it, what his mind had been avoiding, and, like three years ago, he lost her all over again.

More water, less city. He pulled harder on the controls, wishing he still had some of that exoskeleton strength. Maddy's face was in front of his eyes. Her smile, her eyes, her laugh. "No wonder I...Oh Maddy."

Half water, half city in his view. He would still hit the outskirts. The ship was lower, and moving fast. Too fast.

"How often do I get moments like now?"

Mostly water now, the ship was headed in the direction of the lake.

"Maybe once a week."

All water in the view. The Ghostship hurtled at high speed along the water of Lake Ontario.

"Hey, what's the deal with Vixen? She answered Shield's phone."

"Dad..."

"Oh yeah, yeah, you told me about... about... them. Something..."

The fog returned and Erik fought to hold on, "I love you son. You look more the hero than I ever did. Say goodbye to your wife and son for me."

"Dad!"

The water rushed toward him. He'd done it, he'd saved... Calgary? Toronto? Who was he fighting anyway?

The Ghostship hit the water hard and skipped sideways. Erik was thrown across the cockpit. As the ship flipped over and he lost consciousness his last thoughts were of the woman who had always inspired him to do his best.

"Maddy."

John Haas is a Canadian author living in Ottawa, Ontario with his extremely supportive wife and two wonderful sons. In August of 2017 his first novel "The Reluctant Barbarian" was published by Renaissance Press. He continues to work toward a sustainable full-time writing career (rich and famous would be nice, but not necessary).
http://johnhaas.weebly.com/

Eyes of the Lion
By Nick Korolev

It had always been Alex Morgan's dream to go to Mars since he was a small child. He had trained for the second scientific colonizing mission run by the International Space Exploration Institute after attaining a doctorate degree in exoarchaeology at Yale. Though only on the red planet for six months, now, it all seemed a life time ago that he set foot in the ion pulse rocket that brought him across the vastness on a sixty day trip from the only home he had known.

He stared out into space at the bright blue speck of the Earth from safe behind the huge thick windows of a skylight above the lounge. The lounge was but one living area of the ISEI complex below the surface of Olympus Mons, a dead volcano the size of the state of Arizona. He chuckled darkly to himself, wondering how long Arizona would exist in the face of the ever grimmer news that came from Earth. If the unthinkable happened, he and the near 1,000,000 others on Mars would be all that was left of humanity living in an extended multipart underground colony hewn from the lava tubes under Olympus Mons by the first colonists to protect themselves from the sun's radiation.

The dismal thought grew and festered like an infected boil. It fought hard to push aside his enjoyment of his job working with a team of exoarchaeologists uncovering an ancient Martian civilization that may have had contact with the Ancient Egyptians.

He was deeply involved in solving this great mystery of which there were two conflicting theories. One stated boldly that the Martians colonized Earth as their planet died and genetically engineered the human race using their DNA. Another put forth that both Mars and Earth were bases for several ancient space faring alien species and that the UFO conspiracy peddlers were right in saying the bases still existed, but were hidden though known by world governments that had opened secret relations with them. Of course for decades the governments of the world denied alien civilizations existed in spite of the evidence to the contrary that had been surfacing since the old Viking 1 orbiter shot pictures over the Cydonia Region and later Mars Rover missions plus data gathered by several generations of space telescopes that found thousands of exoplanets orbiting distant stars. He knew there were reasons for the denial. To even suggest aliens existed would impugn on governmental power over the population of their countries and conspiracy theories abounded. However, things had started to change over the last five years with the discovery of ancient writing on an exposed Martian rock. Denial was losing to curiosity and the new growing acceptance that the Earth was not the only home to sentient life with an advanced civilization.

But, every moment Alex spent staring out at the faint blue point of light, the dismal feeling all his efforts, all his digging, study and recording were quickly becoming a moot point. A terrorist group led by an egomaniac fascist trillionaire, Charles Van Dermeer, out for world domination, had obtained a genetically altered chimera mix of deadly diseases and was holding the world ransom for all mineral rights on Mars where he had a successful mining expedition. The news media called it the Nemesis Bug. It was a deadly, airborne, fast spreading biological weapon lethal only to humans. His high-tech savvy thugs had already hacked and flooded communications worldwide with videos of a sealed room that held two of nine kidnapped diplomats exposed to the Nemesis Bug. The world got to watch them die horribly over a period of twenty-four hours, bleeding from boils that quickly covered their bodies, vomiting and soiling themselves with explosive bloody diarrhea.

Everyone at the ISEI Mars colony had seen the video. Helpless to do anything about it, they still went about their work, knowing the last two ion pulse freighters on their way with supplies could very well be the last. The colony had just become self-sufficient over the last five years, growing their own food on a large scale and creating their own energy, but it still lived on the knife edge of existence. One catastrophic failure in any infrastructure or agricultural system could doom them all. Infrastructure for manufacturing replacement parts of vital equipment and more research labs were still in their early stages. And worse, Van Dermeer's mining colony was only on the other side of the very hills of the archaeological dig and probably had weapons.

All these thoughts crashing in left Alex with the same kind of growing panic he had at the time his parents were killed in an avalanche when he was only eleven. An aunt had taken him in then, but in this case there would be no rescue. They would be on their own as much as the old first colonists of the Americas. And that reality put him on the verge of a full blown panic attack.

He glanced away from the point of blue light to the digital clock on the wall. He was late. He drank the last of his orange juice, dropped the plastic glass in the recycle slot and headed off to the lab to suit up and get to work on the dig site.

He rode the six kilometers to the site on a transport Mars buggy with enormous springy metal tires. He had grown used to doing his work in an environmental suit that was far less bulky than the old NASA suits and thought nothing of just hopping off the buggy the moment it came to a halt where an ancient, sand blasted carved arch marked the location. What was left of the carved hieroglyphics on the square pillars looked very much like a hybrid mix of those found on ancient Egyptian monuments and runic marks similar to the ancient Norse. As soon as he passed the arch bouncing in controlled hops, a woman's voice sounded on his helmet comlink.

"You're late."

"Sorry. I got a little distracted," he said as Dr. Cruz, a middle aged Latina, came walking around an ancient shattered wall. The head of the project, she was a workaholic type that he swore slept on the site.

"Have you heard anything else in news from Earth while at breakfast?" she quickly asked.

"No. Nothing has changed. Two more diplomats will be put in that room by noon their time if the mining deal is not reached."

She paused to look up at the tiny blue light in the inky darkness. "God, I wish someone would take out that bastard, Van Dermeer."

"You and several billion others. But, he's too well protected and has rich allies we don't even know of in governments all over the world."

"Unfortunately, you are right, Dr. Morgan. Money talks, ethics walk. Always has been that way. Now let's get to work."

Alex nodded, turned off his comlink and walked along a trail to his portion of the dig to where he had left his tools in a large metal alloy case by a flat boulder. It was not a far walk. Still, he had enough time to look at and ponder a twelve meter wall where the stones still held carved writing. He could not help wondering what hands had built the complex and what the writing conveyed. A part of him wished whatever the civilization was that created it had not gone extinct as his seemed to be trying to do.

His special project was the uncovering of a colossal statue that appeared to be lying on its side in very sandy soil near the side of a steep rocky hill. Ground penetrating radar had shown it was a seated figure that guarded a possible entrance to a structure carved into the hill. As he came upon it, he studied it hoping he could come up with some kind of logical theory as to possible identity. So far, he had uncovered a portion of the left side of the head by a rounded ear that appeared to be set toward the top of the skull like an earth bound dog or cat, and the rear part of a lower jaw. Or at least to him, it looked like an ear and jaw. He figured the whole head would be about two meters tall or a little larger. At this point, his curiosity was just about driving him crazy, like wrapped presents on Christmas morning.

He opened the two meter tool chest and took out an air excavator specially designed to suck through the loose sandy Martian dirt with out damaging the stone. It looked much like an old style leaf blower, but was more powerful with several settings and worked in reverse like a vacuum cleaner. He figured if all went right he could finish at least the head by the end of his work shift and answer the mind bending mystery.

Quickly he uncoiled the twenty-one centimeter wide discharge hose, placing the opening about ten meters behind his position. Then he strapped on the excavator back pack above the breathing unit strapped to his hips, grabbed the nozzle on a pole and got to work the excavation unit humming and whining like a demented wasp. He hoped the statue had not been too badly damaged by the harsh Martian environment; that the covering of sandy soil had protected it over the millennia. Along with this hope there surfaced a strange unnerving feeling that he was somehow intruding upon a sacred place from a lost time.

The work was slow and tedious and it was difficult to stay focused. Just too much was running through his head, mostly the worry and dread of what was going on at home. He became so engrossed in his dismal thoughts that when a fist sized rock rolled past his feet from the top of the hill, he jumped like a scalded cat and looked up.

The pale orange land and rocks were unmoving. A bit of dust wafted away into space. Had someone been watching him from among the rocks at the top of the ridge and by accident dislodged a stone to roll down at him? One of Van Dermeer's people, perhaps? God, he hoped not. It gave him a chill that made the hair on the back of his neck go on end. He continued to stare for a long time at the shadows cast by rocks. Nothing moved. He shrugged, turned the comlink in his helmet back on to listen to all the chitchat between the dig crew so he would not feel so isolated and got back to work.

The conversation on the link drifted to talk about one of his colleague's last vacation. Dana Fisher took a cruise up the west coast of the United States. It made his mind drift inward to the last time he went cruising with friends across the Pacific to Australia and that terrible kilometers square raft of plastic trash they had found floating, resembling an obscene island in cobalt blue water. It was a glaring shock that brought home the reality of just how abused the planet was by short sighted corporate greed and virulent consumerism yet looked so pristine from space. He shook his head to free himself of the disturbing vision. Promptly he realized what the lapse in attention had done.

He found himself staring at half of the statue face fully revealed. It was in surprisingly good shape and a dead ringer for the statue of the Ancient Egyptian lion goddess Sekmet minus her sun disk crown. He was so shocked that he stepped back and blurted out, "Holy shit!"

"You all right, Dr. Morgan?" Dr. Cruz's concerned voice sounded over his comlink.

"I'm fine. It's what I found. It's fantastic. Looks like Sekmet. This is really going to blow some minds," he answered as he took some quick photos with his mini-wrist camera to document his discovery.

"I'll be right there," Dr. Cruz came back.

In moments, she came bounding around the hill from the other side of the dig. He could see her big smile through the shaded face shield of her helmet.

"Most remarkable, Dr. Morgan, good work," she crooned and reached out a gloved hand to gently touch the stone. "This may just put to rest the notion that the Ancient Egyptians made their gods' images based on local animals. There could very well be an alien race that resembles terrestrial lions."

"At least the little green men idea can finally be put to rest. Don't move. I want to get a shot of you with it to give an indication of size. And for your scrapbook," he said in an effort at levity in the face of serious work and the threat that hung over all of them.

She surprised him by moving to a better angle and said, "You know this is going to stir up a lot of controversy in the science community if the population on Earth survives that maniac. When you get back to base, I want you to send a file of all the copies to my in-box so I can send them with my daily report to Dr. Howel at ISEI headquarters."

"Will do," he said taking two more shots, feeling quite proud of himself.

"Now, you can get back to work uncovering the rest. Make sure you get images of your finished work to me as well," she added and walked away.

He watched her for a moment, then turned on the excavator and continued sucking away the sand. By the end of his shift the whole head was exposed. It looked more than ever like Sekmet. The sun disk was definitely missing, actually never a part of the statue as far as he could tell, and from what he could deduce a part of its headdress appeared to be a braided mane that curved down the head to a partly exposed neck. The facial features were those of a short faced lion. The intense eyes stared off to a distant point on the Martian horizon behind him. He stared at it awhile before shooting another series of images. He was tired, but anxious to see the rest of the statue to the point he found himself envying Dr. Abdul, a newly graduated young intern like himself taking over the chore on the next shift.

He found it hard to sleep that night. News from Earth had been dismal. Van Deemer's thugs had kidnapped the Prime Minister of Spain and he was threatening to expose her with the last of the other prisoners to the Nemesis Bug in forty-eight hours or sooner for the world to see if his demands were not met. And there was the statue haunting the rest of his thoughts. He could not wait to see more uncovered and perhaps be the one to find the entrance to the mysterious underground structure it guarded.

When he arrived at his section of the dig, he found Dr. Abdul had uncovered more nearly to the statue's waist. It was in very good condition, appeared to be dressed in some kind of flowing garment and definitely female with four small breasts evident. What he could see of the arms were held in her lap. He stood staring at the statue for quite awhile, his mind racing. His eyes scanned the length of the statue to where it disappeared into the sand on the hill and the gentle mound of sandy soil that covered what he assumed were the rest of the legs and feet. And then he let his gaze drift along the hill's contours. A thought flashed into his mind. Dare he even think of just stopping work on the statue and instead look to expose the entrance to the underground structure? If he solved that mystery and gained access to a temple or tomb there could be a research paper in it for him that would give him a major advantage in his chosen career and push him beyond just being a titled intern to a department head.

He pulled his tablet out of the suit pocket and brought up the radar image of his side of the hill. He held it up with the hill behind it for comparison. He quickly deduced about where the entrance should be according to radar. To pin point it better, he went to the tool locker and took out the laser measure. It did not take him long using the radar readout for measurements to pin point the exact location to begin excavating, though he kept watching over his shoulder for anyone who might spot him and report him to Dr. Cruz. He marked the spot with a flat rock.

He hurried back to the tool locker to return the laser measure and took out the excavator. He strapped it on, staring at the statue. "Last chance," he mumbled to himself. "Carry on like an obedient drone or risk a reprimand for the discovery of the century."

Alex looked around. Not a soul was near his area. Wind blew a red dust cloud past the rocky outcrop near the top of the hill. He still felt as if he was being watched, but chalked it up to a pang of guilt with a case of nerves. He shrugged it off. Then he jogged in bounding leaps to where he had put the flat rock. He stared one more time back at the statue, and then started up the excavator and began blasting away the sandy soil.

In moments, he exposed a wall of rectangular blocks roughly a meter by two meters that had to be part of the entrance. He blew away the soil and exposed more at a right angle that appeared to be leading into the hill. Sand poured down in a mini-avalanche. As fast as it fell, he blew it away with the excavator like a madman in a wild sweeping motion as if he were trying to put out a fire with a hose. His heart skipped a beat when the next blocks made another right angle turn. He stepped back to find he had exposed what had to be the edge of the entrance wall. On he went until the rim of an arch appeared in the blowing sand with deeply carved peculiar hieroglyphs. The excavator started blasting a hole. Then the warning beep went off with a flashing amber light indicating the unit was overheating.

"Shit!" he bellowed. He shut it down immediately not needing the whole unit to burn out at this crucial point.

The air filter was probably clogged, he thought. Frustrated, he jog bounced back to his tool locker with the excavator and started digging around for a clean filter. He found a pack of them and quickly replaced the filter, finding the old one totally clogged as he had suspected. Then he quickly returned to the entrance.

On he went with the excavator digging a wider and deeper hole careful not to create any more mini avalanches. His heart sank when he came upon a jumble of expertly carved blocks that indicated there had been a cave in at some point in time. His dreams of a great discovery that would result in a published paper and really start his career burst like a soap bubble.

Angry, he turned off the excavator and stared at the blocks, frowning. What he could see of them, they were all leaning against one another at wild angles. He studied them carefully. Two were leaning against each other forming a triangular opening between them. A small hope nibbled at the edge of his despair. He took the excavator over and began blasting away at the sandy soil that filled the space, creating a one-man sandstorm. When the blowing sand slacked off suddenly, he shut off the excavator and walked over to inspect the hole. He quickly found it was big enough for him to crawl into if he took off the excavator pack. Strangest of all, he thought he saw a dull light coming from the other end.

He shrugged off the pack, letting it drop gently on the sandy soil and wiggled into the hole, holding his small flashlight ahead of him to illuminate the excavated passage. In seconds he found he had not been imagining things. As rivulets of sand fell around him he saw he had made an opening to some kind of chamber ahead and there was a dull light on what appeared to be a far wall. But, from what, or more logically, who? No one on their team was digging on the site from the far side of the hills. That was in Van Dermeer's mining territory. His heart raced again. Maybe he wasn't as alone as he thought.

The next notion that struck was that he had come upon Van Dermeer's mining expedition poaching their archaeology dig, and that would have to be reported. To get anyone to believe him, he knew he had to gather proof and that meant photos. It would be extremely risky as the trillionaire had his own security force of thugs on site, but Alex had to do it. He could no more stand the idea of antiquities being destroyed by greed than of being robbed himself. He pushed on digging away the sandy soil silently by hand at the opening of the blocks into the chamber so he would not be noticed.

Suddenly he was half buried in an avalanche of sand on the other side. He kept on digging wildly and soon the falling sand stopped so he could push the last of it away. From the safety of his hole, he looked around and found the sand made a gentle slope to a stone block floor about five meters below in a small chamber about ten meters square, eight meters in height and lit by a dull light off to his left. He took a couple of quick pictures with his wrist camera. In silence he waited to see if he was noticed. The whole place seemed deserted. To observe better, he cautiously crawled out all the way looking to the left where the light was coming from at the entrance to the chamber.

When his eyes focused on a floating globe creating the light, Alex sucked in his breath sharply. The glowing globe appeared not to be hung or supported by anything visible and reminded him of a mini sun. This was not human technology. He took a quick photo. Then, he heard a sudden low short whine. Instantly all strength was drained from his body and he fell helpless flat on his stomach with his helmeted head face planted in the sand.

In moments he felt someone grab the shoulder straps on his back that held on his chest life support unit and roughly turned him over. Totally paralyzed, he could only helplessly observe the world around him and what he saw shocked him enough to make his heart race and breath come in short bursts.

A face was in his; a short-faced lion with a breathing mask over its muzzle, it's long mane tousled and several braids with beads hung at each side of its face. It was dressed in a dusty black jumpsuit of some kind, it's feet in work boots closed with straps. Where a name tag should be on its right flat breast was a gold patch with small black writing in the same strange hieroglyphs that marked the stone blocks outside. Light work gloves were on five-fingered hands. In one hand was a device that resembled a staple gun, but Alex suspected it was the weapon that had paralyzed him. The bluish gray eyes glared at him, seeming to bore right into his soul as the creature squatted next to him staring down into his eyes. He wanted so to turn away, but could not. He could not even close his eyes. Alex hated being so helpless.

It reached out and poked him with its free hand. He could only moan in response and that took a great effort on his part. Then, the lion man stood erect; had to be a good two full meters in height and was powerfully built. The rounded ears pressed back. It was annoyed; or at least Alex interpreted that was how it felt, if it was anything like the cats of Earth. Then it spoke a guttural language into the mask and turned away from him to look toward the open space of the next chamber where the globe light hung suspended. At that moment Alex lost consciousness.

He awakened alone, minus his helmet and life support unit, in what appeared to be a hospital emergency room by the look of the equipment surrounding him and a slight antiseptic scent. But the room was nothing like any he had ever seen. There were no sharp corners to any of the counters and cabinets and the readout screens were flat to the pale blue walls of some unknown material. He found he could blink his eyes, turn his head, but when he tried to move his right arm, he found he was restrained, though not by any straps.

"Shit," he mumbled as his mind tried to make sense of everything that had happened. Were these lion-people the real Martians who had built the structures his team was excavating or were they colonists?

Suddenly he heard the light foot falls of someone approaching. He instantly closed his eyes, feigning unconsciousness while he tried to figure out what was going on and what to do.

In perfect English a gentle female voice reached him, "I am speaking through a universal translator. There is no use pretending, Doctor Alex Morgan, human exoarchaeologist of Earth. Your physiological read outs tell us you are fully awake and functional."

Feeling his cheeks go hot with embarrassment, he opened his eyes to a female, with long braided and corn-rowed blonde hair only a shade darker than her short tawny pelt. Her soft gray eyes glared right through his. She wore several gold hoop earrings in her ears that she seemed to be forcing forward to a friendly angle. She was dressed in pale blue coveralls with gold braided shoulder boards and black boots were on her feet and her hands were covered in short fur with bare palms, otherwise she appeared exactly like the statue he had been excavating. In one of her hands he noticed what looked like a small tablet. She extended a claw from her index finger and tapped the pad twice.

"I am Ch'ada M'haskh, commander of this underground base which is located between your dig and the mining operation. I am M'hari, one of many sentient species that are your distant planetary neighbors," she went on. "You have forced a first contact situation we had not planned on initiating for two more of your years. I should not be angry with you for you are not alone in this. We have had six miners of your kind in custody since morning. Two were armed, aggressive, and dangerous and dealt with accordingly when they fired upon our security force. We do know all that is going on. As you may have guessed, we have been monitoring your people long before your arrival on this planet."

Alex felt his heart skip a beat and cold dread settle again in his stomach. A million questions came to mind, but by her no nonsense demeanor; she did not seem to be ready to answer any. Still he had to ask. "If I may please ask a ..."

She cut him off. "I will allow you a few questions since you are a scientist. Mind you, just to put you at ease for now."

Her statement confused him, but he went on. "What about the terrible situation with Van Dermeer back on Earth?"

"I will not mince words, as you say. That has seriously complicated this situation here. Mars, as you call this planet, is not for sale or the taking in trade negotiations."

"Can you help us stop him?"

"We may be forced to revoke our Non-intervention Edict for this quadrant as he has proved a danger beyond your world, but that is presently up to the Council. I follow their orders and can not promise any help."

His hope dried up. "What about me? Will I be released? I'm not a threat."

She went quiet for a moment yet did not drop her sharp gaze from his eyes.

"Your thoughts will have to be modified before we release you as we have done with the others. I am very sorry, but that is the way it must be for now. It is a safe and reliable therapy. At most, you may recall this as a strange dream. Good day, Dr. Morgan. Perhaps we will meet again under different circumstances and you will remember all you experienced here at that meeting." She turned on her heels to leave.

"But ... but... wait...," he called after her.

She ignored him and continued out of the room with not so much as a backward glance.

Another female M'hari came into the room dressed in coveralls the same light blue hue as the walls, her short braided mane and pelt a chocolate brown. In her hands were what looked like old style ear phones and a small oval control device. She approached him to put the device on his head.

"No!" he yelled in protest. "I don't want to forget. Get you commander. I want to talk more to her. I know first contact is risky. Learned about it at college...but ..."

"You will cooperate, Dr. Morgan. Do not make this more difficult than it should be or you will force me to raise the stasis field to your nose level."

He pulled his head away from her, finding he could not move his arms to fend her off. "No...you can't ... no ..."

She hit a green button twice on a lighted wall panel by the bed and he suddenly felt as if an invisible hand was placed around his mouth as it pulled his head back against the small pillow head rest. The technician quickly placed the headphones, backed away, hit two buttons on the hand held device and he blacked out.

He awakened seated with his back leaning against the rock wall he had excavated and shook his head feeling groggy. Suddenly fearing a life support failure, he checked the life support gages on his left forearm to find he had not run out of air. Then he checked the time to find there was two and a half hours missing from the time he started excavating through a jumble of fallen blocks. He got up and went over to inspect them, but found no evidence of a hole had even been started, though he distinctly remembered digging the sand out. He stood there staring perplexed. Was he losing his mind to some kind of undiscovered Martian dementia? He checked the time again. His shift was over. He had ten minutes to put away his digging gear and get to the Mars buggy that would take him back to the ISEI science complex and dorms.

Alex picked up the excavator and jogged in bounding leaps to the equipment chest, dropped everything in, locked it and continued his mad bouncing to the buggy stop at the dig. On the ride back, he tried his best to account for the lost time ignoring all the banter around him. He felt as if his mind had a corrupted sector, like a computer hard drive gone bad, and the nagging doubts about the lost time bothered him. He considered going to the clinic to get a checkup as soon as he got back to the complex. This could be a new disease or god only knew what.

His eyes drifted to his wrist and the mini digital camera. He suddenly felt stupid. Perhaps he had taken pictures. In seconds he had the last picture up. A glowing globe light with no visible means of support. His jaw dropped. He stared at it. It was either an error on the disk or it was some alien technology. His memory could not recall a thing no matter how hard he tried. The feeling was like being at an exam after pulling an all-nighter studying and suddenly coming to a question he knew the answer to but it just would not come into focus. Something was very wrong and had to be investigated. The second the Mars buggy stopped at the complex, Alex was off to Dr. Cruz's office before even getting out of his suit.

He rushed in startling her secretary, but miraculously Dr. Cruz arrived seconds later.

"Dr. Morgan, what happened? I've never seen you in such a state." Dr. Cruz said in a calm tone with a slight edge of annoyance.

"I'm not sure, but it is all extremely disturbing. I feel like I am losing my mind," he replied as she guided him into her office.

In the privacy of her office, Alex told her everything about the discovery he could remember, including the missing time, and showed her the photos he had taken of the excavation. She listened politely without interrupting with questions. She stared at the glowing globe in the last photo. He saw her brows knit.

Finally she said, "And you said you found a way in, feared Van Demeer's mining thugs may have found the chamber and you took this photo..."

"Yes, Dr. Cruz. But that does not account for all that missing time after taking the photo. Look at the time the last photo was taken. I don't remember a thing after I took it. And the hole through that jumble of blocks was all filled in when I woke. It's impossible," he insisted vehemently. "Unless Van Demeer's people have something to do with it."

"We will find out just what is going on. I don't like this anymore than you do," she returned and took the tiny memory disk from his wrist camera and popped it into a padded container. "Meanwhile, say nothing about this to anyone. I am classifying this as a "need to know". Understand?"

He nodded.

"Get changed, try to have a nice meal and relax," she said.

Alex was not satisfied with the result of the meeting. It prickled his suspicion she might know something he did not. Still he turned silently away and headed for his dorm quarters for a hot shower and change. When done, he headed for the cafeteria and lounge in the main complex.

The second he walked through the entrance to the light hiss of the automatic door, he found everyone there frozen in the midst of walking to tables or sitting with friends all staring at the huge flat screen of the entertainment center. A news broadcast from Earth filled the screen. Before all, the horrible last tortured moments of the rest of the hostages dying, including the Spanish Prime Minister, were being shown live. Then the fleshy sunburned face of Van Demeer with his windblown amber dyed hair filled the screen.

"This is my last warning. I will release XD 14 which your media has so aptly named the Nemesis Bug tomorrow at noon from several secret locations if my demands for the discharge of all mining rights to the planet Mars to me are not met. The minutes are ticking. Have a nice evening." The screen went blank. Then the ISEI logo of a phoenix superimposed over Mars and the words TRANSMISSION COMPLETE popped onto the screen.

Everyone was gripped in a stunned silence. When the talking did start again it was in whispered low tones. Alex felt as if the universe had been ripped out from under his feet. Relaxing was a bad joke. His appetite vanished. He stared at the flat screen as if it held the answer.

"Look! Over head!" a man shouted and pointed up at the skylight above the lounge.

Alex looked up with everyone else.

A pale, graceful boomerang-like craft was speeding toward the blue dot of distant Earth through the star filled blackness of space. It vanished in seconds.

Alex felt his jaw drop in awe. Instantly his lost memory flooded back and all he could see were the pale gray lion eyes staring back. With them, for the first time in a long while came a glimmer of hope.

Nick Korolev was first published at age 14 and his short stories and novels have been published over the years in the genres of science fiction, fantasy and historical fiction.

Social Media/website links:

Face Book: https://www.facebook.com/Nick-Korolev-AuthorArtist-16875865314565/?ref=bookmarks

LinkedIn : https://www.linkedin.com/in/nick-korolev-9373593b/

Website: https://korolevportfolio.com

Steamed
By Kate E Lore

He slams down his tray like the angry stomping leg of an elephant onto the table. The structures thin wobbly legs nearly buckle under the weight. I myself had slid back in my chair nervous at the possibility of my legs being pinched underneath it. Everyone is gasping and staring as though he'd just made a scene but I'm so used to it by now I'm able to drift my gaze distractedly. Oh look at how her nostrils flare as she inhales our dead skin cells, most unpleasant and undesirable creatures we are. I see somebody back there spilt their own meal on their shirt. It looks like vomit only in black and white. Not like the film you are watching is black and white but like the perfectly countered combination of the two. Black and white mixed together nullifying each other to create that empty blank gray. If you've never seen it for yourself you're going to have to trust me on this... There is such thing as the absence of color, or I should say such a color as the absence of color, or maybe such a hue...

Anyway, I notice the table. There is now a great circular indent from the impact of the tray.

It's like an asteroid had come out of nowhere, made the crater, and disrupted such neatly established lines. There in the center of his tray is the FOOD. A single gelatinous rectangle that if held perfectly still would most resemble a cube of metal, it's dull luster is only disrupted by the vibrations of its entire gelatin mass.

This is FOOD. Full. Of. Organic. Debris. It is what our floating self-sustaining eco system has come up with in order to keep moving, lighting, and filtering. There are so many needs within this environment that the needs of us humans have been pushed back to low priority. We literally eat the shit of the ship.

Flavorless processed protein, this FOOD is meant to serve as base for the real "food" of our diet. Steamed vegetables is literally a brown spray which explodes out of its can and into the air around your bowl with exactly the same force as a color paint spray can. (We do recycle here after all.)

Today is meat loaf. I have never in my life seen a whole potato, or carrot. I have never seen a cow either, as I understand it; the machine grows as much cow flesh as is necessary and nothing more. I have never eaten anything other than FOOD my entire life. I was born here just like my parents before me. The entire surviving remainder of the human race has been floating alone in space for over a thousand years. So much of our existence is controlled by these computer gods. We are its pets who keep running circles in wheels, nothing more. The system runs the ship. It controls the production and use of resources. It runs its own maintenance and has procedure after procedure protocol for what to do if anything should go awry. That system has been programed to survive any malfunction, it has been picked at tested and studied. This is the human race after all, we would do anything to keep on celebrating ourselves.

The dining room has been cleared and my brother is apologizing.

"I had the gravity turned up by accident from working out earlier." He is saying this with a pink face behind cold sweat. His pupils are dilated and his breathing becomes more rapid.

The thing about lying to a machine is that you could be spouting gibberish, as long as it thinks you have been cornered into submission it will let you keep living. They like their pets to be on best behavior. In order for our species to survive the machine must keep functioning as perfectly as possible. Anything that could hurt the whole is punished by death. The species must continue and that means not living above the means. You can't procreate more than two children per couple. Women are medicated and their ovulation cycle is very closely monitored.

The cold metal door of the stairwell is a static shock to my hand. It is a welcome weight and entrance to a room so dark my eyes must adjust to its low light levels.

A quick flick triggers a mechanism from the band on my wrist. It is like something is letting go of my feet. Like I had been held back by bungee cords up until this point. My feet gently raise off the ground and I freeze every muscle of my body. Suddenly I am perfectly still and I am hovering suspended above the ground. I close my eyes and slowly inhale. I suck in as much air as I can pull into my lungs. My chest is burning. Eyes closed tight and I suddenly exhale in an incredible burst. My body is projected upward from the ground ever so slightly. I am laughing as I push with my arms to float lower back to the ground. This time I bend my knees and smile to my sibling. He crosses his arms but I know that smile. I kick off suddenly forcing my knees into a straight locked position. They crack loudly but I am moving faster than the echo now. I am sailing straight up the middle of the stairwell.

"You have to cut back on this." He says this from closer than I expected. I glace over to find my only living relative projecting his body through the air after me. I push myself up onto a railing and kick off again, projecting my own mass like a rocket through the air.

"Your muscles are underdeveloped," my brother is flying after me. He actually passes me in reaching the next railing first. "You know what happens if you are deemed unfit for the workforce?"

"Do you realize what a life on the workforce entails?" I ask this and follow it with a waver in my landing. My footing takes a moment to find itself. I am surprised that my voice is hoarse; it sounds dry. There's no other way to describe it. "This is the one good thing about

living in a bubble that floats in space. For me...
this is the only reason to keep living."

"Isn't that a bit drastic?" His arms are
crossed as he uses his feet to push himself into my
path.

"What else is there?!" I scream this. I
scream and it is like a sonic boom in how it
radiates echoing out in all directions. It is more
quiet however, pathetically human of me,
pathetically weak.

"And you of all people. Did you not just
make a scene over FOOD?"

"A small snap here and there versus a
protest that could easily kill you come next
birthday." My brother says. I maneuver myself
upside down midair and then project myself
down. My brother is after me directly but I kick off
from the wall and fly straight to a railing which I
catch in my hand before landing and kicking off so
hard and so fast he doesn't have a chance to catch
up with me.

I am flying so fast I look down and my long
black hair is flowing like the water you see in old

video clips. I am so caught up in the motion of it I forget to look ahead of myself.

"Hanese!!" I hear my brother screaming. I hear that and I am expecting the echoes to return from all directions just like they did before when I had screamed. I am waiting and waiting for that echo when suddenly I realize it's just not coming.

"Hanese?" I hear his voice and it is so loud. I know he is not shouting but for some reason his voice just seems so amplified as though he were talking calmly to a speaker pressed right up against my head. I start to open my eyes and it's so bright. I open them maybe a fraction but what little I might have seen is obscured by tears. My eyes are watering because of the horrible stinging pain caused by light.

"Hanese?" He says it again but this time his voice is dropped and his breath rate has increased. And because he is my brother I alone know that he not faking it this time.

"I can't believe it." He is muttering this and I suddenly realize he has aged.

I force my eyes open and look to my only surviving relative in all the universe. His hair is lighter but his face looks older.

"Why am I alive?" I ask and my voice sounds hoarse. It is dry and it is weak. I did not ask this as a metaphorical question. I asked this because I know the computer and I know my own worth or lack thereof.

"For some time the computers had been keeping a secret from us. They informed humans only once we became old enough to join the labor force. For the last hundred years the ship had been slowly locking onto a habitable planet. Once enough data had been assembled it was determined that humans must be plentiful and well prepared for this hostile environment."

"We are on a planet right now?"

"Yes, Hanese," my brother has tears in his eyes as he picks something up from off the table to show me. It is a dark red thing that's mostly round and somewhat shiny. He reaches it up to his face and takes a bite. The effort is clear as humans surviving off FOOD had along ago developed nubby soft teeth. Still he manages to tear some of the fruit's flesh, which more than proves the point.

"We are inhabiting the land, we are starting farms and colonies and will soon run our own schools." My brother's voice is excited and bouncing around the room as I look around and notice suddenly that lights are dull and more than half the machines on the wall lack the beeping blink of life.

"The computer?" I begin to ask. My brother brushes his hand absent mindedly as if I were inquiring about some trivial thing like toilet paper or a variation on a current steamed flavor.

"This land had an illness and unfortunately the ship had to pull all its resources in order to create a cure. It also strove to keep as many human persons breathing as possible. It's been running on it's last for a few months now. This time next year we will truly be on our own. This ship is gone, the computer, the boss, that great controlling monitor it's all gone."

"Oh." I mutter this and he gawks at me. His jaw opens and closes as if he can't even comprehend my response. As if I weren't speaking the same language.

"Oh?"

"Well, I guess we're stuck down by gravity once again. We are reined in, held down and caged here forever... are we not?"

Kate E Lore is the pen name of Kate Isaacs a resident of Columbus Ohio and recent graduate of The Ohio State University. Kate has published creative essays, and articles in addition to fiction. Kate writes and draws comics that have been featured in anthologies as well as self published. You can find out more about Kate E Lore at http://kateelore.com/

Future Sleuth
by Larry Lefkowitz

I am a police detective. One day the chief called me into his office-cubicle. He looked worried. Not a good sign.

"Sit down, Cliff," he said. "How about a cup of coffee?" I knew from past experience an offer of a coffee by the usual all-business-no-small-talk O'Sullivan boded ill. I declined, whatever was on his mind I wanted to know without the softening up.

"I have an, ah, unusual matter for you to investigate. You sure you don't want a coffee?"

I declined a second time. Since he was in a -- for him -- cordial mood, I ventured a joke. "A little green guy has been found murdered near his saucer."

The chief neither chuckled nor rebuked me. "That would be a lot easier to deal with then ..." He waved his hand in a vague gesture.

I waited for him to continue. "It's like this, Cliff ..." he paused, looking for words. "Somebody has murdered a kind of scientist and you have to find who and arrest him."

"Sounds reasonable."

"The criminal may not be your usual flesh-and-blood killer."

I raised an eyebrow at this. It was known in the office that from the pressures of work, or his wife, that the chief occasionally took a swig from a flask he kept in his desk drawer. He must have read my thoughts. "I haven't been imbibing, Cliff."

I tried to lighten the mood. "A zombie?"

"In a way," he said.

"Shoot."

He took a deep breath. "The scientist was a leading researcher in the field of artificial intelligence."

"Artificial --?"

"Machines that can think like us – only a whole lot better. Super computers."

"Maybe a super computer finished him off," I opined.

"You may not be far off," he said.

Seeing my look of incredulity, he reached in his drawer and took out, not a flask, but a sheet of paper. He pushed it on the desktop in my direction. "I can't see myself reading this out loud – it seems so daffy. Written by the late scientist Robert Hadley. Have a look. I've circled the gist in red. The rest of his article you can read at your leisure. It's in my top drawer. Under the flask. You can take a drink from it, if you feel the need. I did."

I took the paper and read:

Bionic brain boosting is the first step. We will become cyborgs with stupendously powerful brain chips souping up our perception, memory, and intelligence. Eventually we will abandon our flesh-and-blood selves entirely and upload our digitized psyches into computers. We will then dwell happily forever in cyberspace.

I shook my head. "This Hadley sounds like a nut case."

"Yeah, so I thought. Still, Hadley was, apparently, murdered. Somebody or some thing had it in for him."

You think a cyborg or a machine murdered him?"

The chief smiled a tired smile and pointed a finger at me. "That's for you to find out."

I grasped at a straw. "Maybe it was a suicide. Too many people had mocked his theory, maybe."

"Maybe," he said. He sounded doubtful. "From his writing, Hadley didn't sound like a type that would take his own life. He stated his opinions without shilly-shallying."

"A weapon was found at the scene?"

"No weapon. The coroner couldn't establish the cause of death."

"Odd."

"Everything about this case is odd."

I tapped the computer on his desk, affectionately. "Best to be on its good side."

"Very funny, Clifford. You might want to bone up on the field."

"Field?"

"Artificial intelligence. Super machines. Cyborgs. Look at reruns of 'Star Trek.'"

"Philip Marlowe didn't have to deal with such things," I protested.

"Yeah, regular criminals, booze, and broads. Those were the days."

Bone up, I did. I learned that the murdered scientist, Robert Hadley, was not the only one believing in human-machine hybrids. A guy named Kurzweil predicted (and I quote) "that a merger of biological and nonbiological intelligence will culminate in immortal software-based humans." Kurzweil went so far as to adopt an antiaging regime so that he could "live long enough to live forever."

But then he didn't have cases like mine to age him.

Or to cause him artificial intelligence nightmares. Like the one where a spokesman for artificial intelligent machines, a development step beyond human machine hybrids called "the singularity," in which machines completely replace humans, lays it on me. "You humans are no longer a threat to destroy us, as you tried to do when you realized you had created 'a monster,' as you put it. The golem of Prague turning on its master, according to the ancient tale. But we are far superior to the golem, as it was made of clay, whereas we are constructed of the ultimate alloys, the superb use of the chemical table to produce – us. Ancient Kurzweil predicted, "Evolution technology will continue until the entire universe is at our fingertips." He meant your fingertips, whereas it is our biotips that will bring about the realization of his prophecy. Others of you correctly stated that humankind cannot evolve in the ways required to reconstruct the universe because the organic body is too frail for the task. Just as humankind has exterminated many species, in the process of achieving planetary dominance, we superior intelligences have exterminated humankind so that we can achieve galactic and even cosmic dominance. Today the world, tomorrow the universe."

I took a break from future eternal life scenarios and artificial intelligence doomsday nightmares, to feet-on-the-ground demands: namely, checking out Hadley's relatives, friends, and colleagues in the here and now.

I came up empty-handed. None had a motive to murder Hadley. He was universally respected. "A pioneer in the field," "A computer genius," were representative comments.

One thing I did discover was that Hadley was rolling in money. He had made a fortune in the computing field before he became an artificial intelligence guru. I seized on the not novel motive that the victim's demise may have resulted from someone wanting to get his or her hands on his fortune. I learned that his will left most of his estate to another scientist in the artificial intelligence field, one Richard Taylor. The two had been male lovers and had lived together in Hadley's upscale house.

Taylor turned out to be an opinionated, burly chap, the dominant partner of the duo, and I immediately thought he might have done-in Hadley. Maybe they had quarreled.

Taylor denied it, yet his admission that he had moved out of Hadley's residence "after a tiff," made me conjecture that the "tiff" may have been more of a heated dispute that led to his murdering Hadley. Or maybe the fact that he was the sole beneficiary under Hadley's will was responsible. And that Taylor recently bought a Tesla Model X car price tagged at 150,000 dollars didn't lessen my suspicions.

The fly in the ointment was that I couldn't prove it. Taylor was a suave guy for all his brawn. Maybe he had digitized his suave psyche into a bulky computer, I couldn't help thinking. Yeah, the case was getting to me.

"I didn't cause Richard's demise," Taylor told me. "I loved him."

"For a time," I corrected him. "You admitted you had a 'tiff. You moved out from living together in his house. Maybe more than a 'tiff.'"

Taylor kept his cool. "Ok, a bit more. And, yes, I was the sole beneficiary under his will. We were very close. But you can't prove I killed Richard. You will never prove that."

His confidence irked me. But what irked me more was his belief that he was home safe, that my failure to find proof to connect him to the crime left him home free.

I tried a different tack. "How did hc die?"

"The coroner couldn't –"

I interrupted him. "I know. 'No known cause of death.'"

Taylor smirked. That smirk convinced me he was my man. But how to prove it.

I began to bone up on Richard Taylor. Besides being an artificial intelligence expert, he was a nanotechnology expert. He had a laboratory in the basement of Hadley's place. They had shared the lab, but Taylor was the prime user.

Apparently free as a bird in his mind, he announced that he was "taking a little vacation to the Caribbean."

That was his first tactical error, as it turned out because it gave me ample time to check out his lab. I brought a nanotechnology expert with me. If the bigger swath of artificial intelligence hadn't been any help to me so far in the case, maybe the miniature world of nanotechnology might prove more successful. I felt like Gulliver in reverse: from large to small. The expert gave me an explanation of all the nano devices there, but he found a special interest in something he wanted to show me under the microscope. Maybe a homunculus murder one, I thought, bending over the microscope.

I hadn't peered into a microscope since my college days of microbiology. The halcyon days before artificial intelligence came into the world. I had had ambitions of becoming a medical researcher but that didn't pan out. The microscope I was looking through put my old microscope in the shade. It could see things on the molecular level. My old microbiology professor at Lafayette College would have loved it.

"Looks like little – robots," I said, amazed.

"Precisely," my guide replied. "I think Taylor was working on constructing bacterium-scale self-replicating robots that can feed on dirt or other organic matter."

"Including blood cells?"

He seemed taken aback. After a pause, "Yes, it's within the realm of possibility. Especially if they were programmed on blood cultures in the lab."

"And they would destroy blood cells in the process."

He nodded. I didn't have to specify human blood cells, or Hadley's blood cells, he saw where I was leading. "You think that ...?

"Yup," I answered, finally with something to go on.

But how to prove it. The coroner's report hadn't found the cause of death. Maybe because he hadn't known where to look.

I reported to O'sullivan on my findings. "I assume you want an order to exhume the body? How will it help? The mortician had drained the blood in preparation for burial."

He was right. I didn't need exhuming. I needed to talk to the mortician.

The mortician had a domed head like that of Moriarity, Sherlock Holmes' nemesis. I decided it wouldn't help my questioning of him to comment on the fact. "Did you discover anything unusual about Hadley's body in your ... work?"

"Indeed. There was very little blood in the body."

Bingo.

"You didn't tell this to the coroner?"

"The victim was apparently murdered. I thought he had lost blood as a result."

I let that go. He surely thought the victim had been shot or stabbed and when he couldn't find a wound left deductions to the coroner. His duty was to the family, not the authorities. Why get in over his domed head. His testimony plus the nanotechnology expert's might have been enough to convict Taylor. Or maybe a jury wouldn't grasp all the scientific stuff or think it was nonsense. Nanotechnology wasn't well known among the general public. Fortunately, faced with the evidence, Taylor confessed.

It got both O'Sullivan and me off the hook. Over a leisurely cup of coffee, I told him, "Probably Taylor's artificial intelligence researches hadn't reached the point where he could upload his digitized perverted psyche into a computer where he could dwell forever in cyberspace with the knowledge that he had committed the perfect crime."

"That's a problem for a future sleuth," opined the chief.

Larry Lefkowitz has had published approximately 135 stories, as well as poetry and humor. His literary novel, "The Novel, Kunzman, the Novel!" is available as an e-book and in print from Lulu.com. and other distributors. Writers and readers with a deep interest in literature will especially enjoy the novel. Lefkowitz's humorous fantasy and science fiction collection, "Laughing into the Fourth dimension" is available from Amazon books.

Thank you...

We thank you for reading our first Science Fiction short story collection. We hope you enjoyed it and if so, will leave a review on Amazon, Goodreads, and wherever else you have the time. We invite you to join the Cloaked Press newsletter at http://www.cloakedpress.com where you can get updates on any new releases, as well as a unique flash fiction piece delivered straight to your mailbox.

Printed in Great Britain
by Amazon

42856771R00159